TOP PRIORITY

Borgo Press Books by DORU TĂTAR

Top Priority: A Science Fiction Novel

TOP PRIORITY

A SCIENCE FICTION NOVEL

DORU TĂTAR

Translated by Petru Iamandi &
Raymond Humphreys

THE BORGO PRESS

MMXI

TOP PRIORITY

Originally published under the title, *Prioritate Zero*

FIRST BORGO PRESS EDITION

Published by Wildside Press LLC

www.wildsidebooks.com

DEDICATION

For My Sons

CONTENTS

FOREWORD
by PETRU IAMANDI

This book was simultaneously a literary debut and the first Romanian post-Revolution SF novel. The priorities, however, are not to be found there. They are foreshadowed by the title and the novel's ideas, although the cover would promise a thrilling action rather than anything else. The book is a presentation, a comment, and a partial extrapolation of the ontological pattern created by Mihai Draganescu in the last two decades and synthesised in *Inelul lumii materiale/The Ring of Material World* (1989). Draganescu's book is a philosophical essay, remarkable in its originality, value, and exhaustiveness, which intends to be and succeeds in being much more than a mere exercise of the spirit.

At a first glance, this book might be regarded as a popularising one. The problems it deals with are much ampler, though. The conflict of ideas is permanent, dense and diversified, and includes most of the questions concerning the human element as existence and becoming, no matter if it is maintained by the microcosm of terrestrial astronauts, the civilisation of a strange cosmic being, or the actions of a supercomputer which surpasses its masters in skills. The plot unravels on several levels which converge in the end to originality, depth, and philosophical tension. The ideas of Mihai Draganescu's *Ortofizica/Orthophysics* (1985) are also skilfully presented and exploited here, pointing to the dimensions of God's creative act. Man's wishes to know and create prove to be eternal human values, extended to the dimensions of the whole rational life in outer space, an excellent motivation for human-kind's exodus towards the stars, its mission being to grasp the secrets of the Universe's existence, to create another Universe and, maybe, other intelligent beings (a perpetual sequence of worlds, in which matter and information cyclically mirror the senses and depth of the rational).

Maybe a more experienced writer would have hesi-tated to approach such a demanding theme. He might have been concerned with exploiting this wealth of ideas and actions in at least two or three novels. He might have taken much more care of his characters, individualising them and abandoning that schematisa-tion—somehow deliberate—which gives them only the role to support conflicting ideas and states. He would have abandoned the precision and sobriety of expression, as if instinctively afraid of not disguising this plebe of ideas.

The solid structuring of the book, the remarkable epic rhythm, as well as its rich imagination, lead the readers through an exciting adventure, with certain scientific elements betraying the technical background of an author who wishes, though he does not admit it, to extend a bridge, by means of SF, between the humanistic cultural universe and the scientific one, foreshadowing a third unifying culture. In this sense, *Top Priority* is an original novel, and a pathfinder in Romanian SF.

PART I

The vaster the power gained, the vaster the appetite for more.

Ursula K. Le Guin

At first, there was nothingness....

Then an explosion of light in his eye sockets, and thousands of living needles invaded Ted's senses.

The indeterminate state of his whole body suddenly gave place to a violent pain. It spread from his brain in a sheeting sea of flames towards his back and limbs. For a moment, the scream of his inflamed nerves mastered everything. Then the powerful shock to his senses changed his solar plexus into a resounding cavity which rapidly seemed to fill his body. It was an explosion that seemed to blow him into distinct pieces, and even the brain pulsed, only at once to stop, to collapse upon itself, leaving behind an ocean of darkness. In this Ted lost himself again.

* * * * * *

"Orm!"

In the immense underground gallery, the call stirred

strange echoes making the buzz of the power installations disappear.

"Orm! The analyser! What're you waiting for?"

The second call had more effect. A long rustle, followed by stifled noises and a dry crack, stirred the far end of the laboratory into life. From the darkness emerged a deformed figure struggling with remnants of installations fastened by tangled wires that clung stubbornly to his soles. The figure stopped every now and then, trying to get rid of these encumbrances, whistling strangely as it made its bizarre progress. The limbs were raised rhythmically in turn, accompanying the grotesque ballet of the suckers in a nervous attempt to liberate the cylindrical body of the being. Its skin wrinkled in waves, witnesses to its evidently nervous state.

"Analysers...," whistled Orm angrily. "Here, take it—the analyser!"

Puzzled, the other Varyan looked at him for a few seconds, then suddenly protested:

"You are a monument to cackhandedness and blundering! I'll never understand what you're doing here in a research unit. You wander about, nose around, and ask about this and that. You understand nothing. More than that, you despoil and mess up everything everywhere. Look!" he went on, rolling his short flat limb on the smoking remnants spread on the floor.

"You've destroyed the only flux analyser we've got here. The only one!"

Orm's reply came straight away, in hurried strident

whistles.

"Big deal! We didn't have a chance of doing it anyway. I've had enough of your impossible ideas. I made it easy for you to get posted to this place because you promised me an epoch-making experiment," said Orm, breathing deeply. "But I think I was wrong. It's not worth the danger I have to face.... The professor can find us here at any time now...." The Varyan's thin antennae stung the air, their undulating top protuberances pointing at the other being, Sit, in a seemingly provocative way. "The analyser's gone. So what? We'll have to start your installation.... You admitted yourself that you were waiting for an opportunity...or are you afraid you might blow it?" Orm continued derisively. Then he finished, triumphantly: "Anyway, it's now or never. I took a risk creating this experiment. You can't deny that, so now I've earned my right to see it in progress. I'm fed up with seeing everyone bumbling about for dozens of cycles hoping that they could bring this creature back to life...if we know what life means to it, that is...."

While the Varyan's whistles continued in their staccato way, his eyes stared back at the container room. Through the transparent walls and the plasma he could discern Ted's body, lying there covered by a web of sensors and wires connected to the floor. Above the Earthling, the ceiling descended in an unusual formation of funnels that surrounded his prone body. These were the fruit of Sit's latest researches—they focused unknown fields whose meaning none of the scientist's colleagues had yet even begun to decipher.

Orm noticed a certain detail that made him forget the funnels. He stared at it intently, then turned to the bench next to him and stood still for a moment. It was as if he was making an attempt at dialogue with the magnetic fluxes of the indicators. Hesitantly at first, then more and more rapidly and precisely, Orm pushed his soles forward and some of the suckers of his limbs started to run over the apparatus. It responded obediently. The Varyan's antennae swirled about him in fanlike waves, betraying indecision. His mouth opened slowly to whistle but he simply forgot to do it and pointed instead to one of the screens. From behind, Sit said forcefully.

"Yes, it's not an illusion. The biofield generators are working."

"So that's where the energy leak was," said Orm, recovering from his surprise. "It's much bigger than the one maintaining vital processes.... I wonder if decomposition would release it at a greater speed...."

But Sit did not seem to be paying attention to what Orm was saying. He continued in an authoritative, almost sententious tone.

"Nothing was in vain: the struggle to decipher the information codes; the effort to reconstruct the mechanisms of metabolic change; the reconstruction of the areas destroyed by the impact; the atmosphere on Var; the stupid experiments of all the incompetents here.... The monster in front of us is alive now. My bioenergy field-codifying matrix has proved correct. Do you realise that this is a unique moment?"

Orm was so elated that his whole body seemed unstable. His soles had moved apart and now tended to rise at the same time. His limbs beat the air in disorderly gesticulations, while the suckers stuck to one another in nervous discharges and made unnatural slurping noises.

After a pause in which he gloated on Orm's reaction, Sit resumed his emphatic mocking tone.

"You all turned against me just because I was a southerner. You removed me from the main research group; you and that incompetent professor of yours. He wanted to destroy the creature so he could analyse its information processing central unit. Idiots! You tried to destroy where I'd always wanted to reconstruct. You'll very soon see how the creature's intelligence can be determined without affecting those tissues whose fineness and organisation go beyond our understanding. According to my theory, the agglomeration of living units," he pointed two of his suckers at Ted's head, "is much more important than that of the information processing charge. In the new program, I'm going to assign a new role to it. Any idea what that will be? No, of course not," he said, with an insinuating smile. "It'll be that of a resonant cavity of the bioenergy field fluxes emitted by me and captured by the creature as external stimuli, transmitted not by the information channels it is accustomed to but directly by the encoding made here." He pointed to what was above the container room.

In this way, Sit revealed his intentions, mixing his words and ideas as if wanting to get his message across without delay. Orm broke in anxiously:

"What? How can you be so sure of the validity of your theory? OK, so deciphering the organisation code of the energy matrix *is* a remarkable achievement. I for one didn't believe in it and still don't understand how you've achieved it. But to stimulate the monster in this way is just too much. No," he whispered as if to himself, "you won't succeed."

"Do you really think that? Look, then!" the scientist shouted, pointing to the indicators on another panel. "That's the witness module. I caught something just as I called you. Pity it happened so fast. I've got the recording, though. Now I'll couple the memorisers and reproduce the phenomenon in an accessible time basis."

Before Orm could say one more word, Sit started to activate the instruments. Then they pressed against each other in front of the tiny screen. Sit sucked in a small sphere from the bench with the tip of one of his hurriedly opened suckers. A strident signal came in response and the indicators of the witness module came to life. The Varyans' eyes stared ahead in maximum concentration. Everything was expectation. Fractions of time units succeeded one another in a mad race. The tension was discomfiting. Sit was making the creature lose control over the various parts of its body. Yes, the being certainly belonged to a common Universe, and his theory looked like it was going to be proved correct. He had introduced stimuli into the creature and had captured their response. What kind of contact had been made, he wondered. And what exactly had the apparatus recorded?

* * * * * * *

As usual, Mag was awakened by the itching wrist of her left hand on which she was wearing the sleep program-regulator. She bent forwards and with a very much reflex gesture took it off. Then she switched the watch-robot to "Watch." Passively, she waited to resume control over her vital reflex functions, responsiveness to stimuli, and finally for the automatic permission to leave the rest area. At last, she was ready to move.

Mag hated this whole class of robots. She felt so humiliated at having to depend in this way on them. She had begun to hate them while still a child. Creativity games, training programs, relaxation programs, the whole of it was invaded by machines. With quietly oppressive competence they offered their services, replacing contact with another human. Later, too stubborn to submit, she made the aversion she felt into a challenge. She was now a space biologist and all her activities spoke of refusal to tolerate the supremacy of machines over living matter. Life was an extraordinary phenomenon, and it had to become again the fundamental object of human research. They were far from having said the final word about it.

The mechanics of life had been unravelled a long time ago, with the fast progress of genetics and bionics at the beginning of space age. The confrontation between Man and machine had taken the most varied and unexpected forms. These were dramatic and military in their consequences sometimes, and this had finally ended in an armistice. And with what result? This complete madness: living matter was yielding submissively to artificial matter, its own creation. An inexorable law of evolution? Whose evolution?

"Mag!"

The face of a delicately-featured young woman had suddenly appeared on the video-monitor.

"Eva," replied Mag in an out-of-sorts tone, "in the long-ago I'd have asked you to knock on the door. Though classic good manners seem old-fashioned now, please try to remember I've always used my personal call sign when contacting you."

"My dear, it's obvious you've just woken up, and I'm intruding on you," said Eva, slightly maliciously. "You're, as always, disarmingly natural. And that's what we all envy you for, your naturalness," she added laughing. "You take no entertainment programs, no intelligence stimulators, no bioenergy pills. No one can say why you live in that way, practising psychosomatic self-control, when there are so many facilities around. Look, I admit, I'm good for nothing without them. Do you know what the others say about the barmy space biologist?" she asked, persisting with her barbs. "That you'll manage to rediscover the nervous diseases of our forefathers, the ones you're trying to live like."

That was too much. Mag's face turned to stone. She

knew her colleagues sniped at her in this way. Under different circumstances, she just might have been interested in what they thought of her, but now....

"Stop! That's enough! You're just risking getting on those nerves of mine," she said spitefully, trying to calm herself. "As for bio-programs, I know they've become a vice with you. You'd be lost without them. I know how much you've been using and reusing them since Ted disappeared.... Poor Tim, he'll soon have half a cyborg for a mother.... By the way, what you told me about him yesterday was absolutely shocking. It could interest us all.... Let's go to B3 Level group room and talk to Dan about it."

If Mag had not switched the video-monitor off in such a hurry she would have seen Eva paling sharply at these last words. Eva and Ted had been an agreeable couple when they were on board the intergalactic ship. He was an explorer, she a reputed specialist in handling expert programs. Their different professions had been compensated by an affectionate equilibrium and a harmonious marriage. They had been the first true couple to have a child on the ship. But implacable destiny had changed everything.

* * * * * * *

Suddenly the impulse was there. The two Varyans watched the response of the apparatus on the monitor. It was lengthening the recording. The response had appeared. Indeed, it had been clearly perceived by the sensors within the container. They were undoubtedly watching the event they had so long been waiting for—one in perplexity, the other with his senses almost unbalanced by emotion. It was an extraordinary moment. For the first time in the history of the Varyans, they saw an artificially-controlled biofield contacting living matter. More than that, the phenomenon had resulted from an evolution foreign to their world. What Sit had managed to do was far beyond anything that any other scientists in the Institute had even been trying to achieve.

These were Orm's last thoughts for, in the following seconds, he saw the verdict displayed by the signal-processing system. It overwhelmed him, making him collapse on the floor. The apparatus showed clearly that the impulse belonged to a creature that, during the contact, had become aware of its own existence. This had happened while they had barely realised that something strange was taking place. Everything pointed to the fact that this was a creature capable of thought.

Orm got over his shock and rose slowly on limbs that obeyed him again, and blocked the access to the laboratory. The stiffness of his movements betrayed what he was about to do. First he stared at Sit for a few seconds, then he went to the console in the wall. He took out a silvery helmet, put it on the other Varyan's antennae, and connected it to a small rectangular box. He switched the system on and started with an emphatic whistle.

"Sit, I know you're lucid. Stop pretending you have some sort of mental block. You must answer my questions. Do you understand?"

The researcher, his will annihilated, fluttered his eyelids slowly several times, covering his big eyes from left to right. Orm looked pleased and went on.

"Sit, does anyone else know about what's been happening in the laboratory?"

This time Sit's eyelids fluttered in a left and right movement with the same robot-like motion.

"Sit, have you ever done this experiment before?"

"Yes," the Varyan managed to whistle.

"Here, in this laboratory?" continued Orm, obviously surprised.

"No."

"With a being from Var?"

"Yes."

"Did the experiment succeed?"

"No."

For a while the only sound Orm could hear was the discreet hum of the installation. Then his antennae contracted and loosened to reach his mouth.

"Sit, both of us know we've got a living creature here, the representative of an intelligent world, one that's possibly superior to our own. The suspicions of the technicians who have analysed the remains of the apparatus found beside it have been finally confirmed. However, from now on, any link between the Institute and the outside world will be strictly controlled. This is a case outside either of our competencies. The prerogatives of my social status, which is above yours, entitle me to make this decision. You'll make a full report on the experiments. By the powers invested in me by the Professor I will closely watch all your movements. As a result of the suspicion and distrust your activity has caused here, you are the victim of your own behaviour. Now you'll have to take a break from it all."

Orm pressed a button on the small box. Almost instantaneously, after a short violent shiver that crossed his body, Sit turned into an inert mass on the slabs of the laboratory. Orm bent over him to check the efficiency of the shock. Then he pulled out one of the antennae, took the small box and went to a trap door that opened and swallowed him up.

Left to their own devices, the curiously winking screens and the faint buzz of the still operating power apparatus talked among themselves in a language that only they could understand.

* * * * * * *

"Yes, Olf, that's the truth! My team's mission has come down to designing the course of the spaceship through this huge galaxy and avoiding the areas which could stop or delay our flight. A speed of half a parsec a second is no joke, especially when you literally don't know where you're going."

Lem's aggressive attitude towards the spaceship captain was not something that was new. Against Olf's experience and authority, the young navigation group leader would set his complete honesty, exceptional training, and the refusal to tolerate without question anyone who wanted the last word. It was more than eight years since he had been guiding the ship through outer space. To this he could add twenty more spent on other ships. Even if he counted the thirty-one years before he had received his navigator's licence, Lem could still say he was a young man. As a matter of fact, he had spent almost eighty years in anabiosis, but they were years when he could not exactly say he had lived. That state, characteristic of long flights, was what half the crew was enduring right at this moment.

On the video-monitor, Lem's face showed a tension that was easy to understand. A bitter grimace showed that he realised his situation. He had crossed the border-line and he was in a tight spot.

Olf was staring at the screen without seeing it. His eyes were focusing on something beyond its surface, as if trying to pass on to it the anxious load of his thoughts. The burden of responsibility made him look about Lem's chronological age. Ever since the main biotronic brain of the spaceship had been rendered useless, he had become the main decision-maker of the expedition. They all knew that Olf was an exceptional astronaut. He had led a number of expeditions and proved his extraordinary skills on many occasions, but the situation now was completely different and challenging, to say the least. For almost a century biotronic brains, which included neuronal tissues in their make-up, had worked at levels far above any exclusively human competence.

A bizarre phenomenon that had revealed itself since they had left the galaxy made the use of the central ordinator impossible. The conception-processing units showed strange signs of mental alienation. The perplexity of the members of the expedition was only matched by the consequences of this. They had lost a lot of time in trying to see what had happened. In the end, their fretting had to give way to a state of resignation. They came to the conclusion that none of the computing units was out of order. It was only the living tissues of the ordinator that could be blamed. One by one, the central information-processing units were left to "talk to one another"—as a bioinformatician had graphically put it. Then all activity was taken over by the level computers and the decision-making cells of the research centre.

The greatest loss was the centralised memory-unit that refused to reproduce the necessary space-time co-ordinates of the flight. The derangement of the living tissues of the unit had caused the data to be transferred in some way. No one knew where and how this had happened within the immensity of the biotronic brain. Without these fundamental elements, there could be no going back for anyone on the ship.

Young Lem's outburst and tone were partly justified by the situation. The human psyche could not accept everything, after all. Olf did know that, but he could not afford to lose control of anything. He replied in an inflexible voice, looking sternly into the navigator's eyes.

"I could tell you you've got a false perception of the situation. There's a certain objective we're heading to, and we haven't got enough data to change our flight co-ordinates. It's true the situation's far from being ordinary but the top priority objective's the same. As for your outburst, it shows confusion, maybe tiredness, and certainly a lack of self-control. Navigator Lem, the Navigation Council will let me know when you've yielded the leadership of your department—and that's to be not later than the start of the next daily cycle."

With a curt gesture, Lem was replaced on the screen by the visual call sign of the Level B central unit.

"This is the captain speaking. I want the update."

Dan appeared on the screen. The look on his rather long face spoke of anxiety. With sudden clumsy movements he had the monitor display a text and said:

"Summon the meeting of the Ship's Council yourself. It's not my proposal, but I do support it."

Olf's eyes rested for a few seconds on the text then stared at the ship's chief.

"What does that really mean? I can't see the connection between what you usually do and this case. And I don't see how such a problem can cause the summoning of a Council meeting. Research has been finished for a long time and, as far as I know, reports will be filed."

"That's right," Dan quickly replied. "The new details seem very interesting to me, though. I'm not an expert in bionics or in information transmission but I can appreciate the value of new data. If you refuse, I'll formally make an appeal to the Council Chamber. My evidence will be taken into account properly. I'm absolutely sure of that."

"All right," said Olf thoughtfully. "You can do it, but I don't want you to summon anything before the next ordinary meeting."

The captain switched the connection off and then went over to the personal control desk. The sensors placed discreetly behind his ears indicated increased tiredness. He had simply been doing too much work. Olf had tiny stimuli placed on his body, along the meridian energy tract that affected the cortex. He had never understood the work of the bioprograms. He felt more comfortable with the old, traditional methods.

The adjoining wall slid slowly back to reveal a network terminal. From that he could learn of any detail concerning the intergalactic ship or the crew's work. With its help he could make his decisions. How long am I still going to work in this place? he wondered. A foggy shadow took hold of his still lively, quick eyes when he remembered his age. Did he want to be useful one more time, to share his huge experience with the others? How much longer could he continue to be a shaper of human destinies? He had deceived Time thousands of times but the illusion of eternal existence was starting to fade away now, giving ground to a cruel reality. The burden of years and changes was getting harder to bear. The eternal fighter's destiny prevented him from giving way. He still wanted to confront the problems of the expedition and of those around him. He had resorted to anabiosis because Time had to be stopped once again. There was a need to spend that time properly. He had been awoken when the biotronic brain had surrendered the management of the ship in good will, despite its bizarre malfunctioning. He felt respect and admiration for its circuits, as much anyway as he could feel such a thing for a machine. Could he now do the same thing as the biotronic brain? The struggle with implacable Time had become grim, pitiless. He had assessed the expedition's chances of survival. They were very few. Had he ever hoped subconsciously that he would not be asked to help? He knew better than anyone that he was not going to take the shock of a new anabiosis. This was going to be his last mission. But, no, he wouldn't give up. He had to follow this all the way to the bitter end.

There was a mission he had to accomplish. Dan's call had sounded like a challenge. He had to get ready to face it. He pressed a few buttons and took out a micro-cassette containing the details of a search of KH-09 solar system in the galaxy they were crossing. Ted's last mission.

* * * * * * *

The galactic nebula was spinning in a direction contrary to the usual one. Its speed was hallucinatory. He was there, in the middle of the stellar cloud which was pulsing regularly, soothingly, warmly. It was good. Heat was the first sensation that he was aware of. It brought with it his first glimpse of consciousness. Why was he hot? The spinning crowded matter around him, making it denser and denser, as if it were being pushed by an outside will. There was something there that suddenly appeared to whirl the original equilib-rium, wiping out the myth of permanence. It was an unknown flux, coming from everywhere and nowhere, as if from another dimension, wont to organise and structure everything. He felt that soon something would inevitably encompass him.

The middle of the cloud of stellar dust was becoming fragmented, condensing into spheres of fire. New swarms of stars thus formed began to surround him, catching him in their dance. From this state verging on an odd vertigo, he perceived his own conscious-ness. He realised with amazement that he might have his own will, provided it was not annihilated by the new rhythm pulsing everywhere. He seemed to be the victim of a confused mix of pleasant sensations fighting an avalanche of troubled states. These he was instinctively trying to avoid. Caught in that chaotic dance, the matter around him seemed to be taking on contours which seemed to be fringing him, as if shaping his being out of nothingness into a parallel space. These strangely allowed him to look at himself from the outside. But he only saw the cosmic vacuum. Was he just a mixture of sensations? Shapeless? No, he felt it, but not around him, just inside himself. That was where he had to look.

His effort was followed by an intense emotion. Something was changing there, irrevocably, some-where at the limits of his own consciousness. It was contracting faster and faster, certain that it would find itself. There, only there, did he have to stop. He soon became a nucleus of intense energy ready to make the leap to matter. Then all exploded in an expanse of intense light. He passed quickly, without hesitation, through the stage of a super-dense plasma ball. Then his senses turned into energy fluxes. Violent currents, different from those of closed circuits, started to outline a body. With myriads of unseen threads he was weaving himself a skeleton which was taking its substance from the vacuum around. Why did he have to create his own identity, an identity insignificant when compared to his belonging to the whole universe, to his identification with the eternal matter, whose only dimension was its own limitlessness? His thoughts were starting to get coherent now, seeming to take shape from the agglomeration of sensations at the same time with the completion of material contours. He was himself now, but in another state. What state? He did not know. Suddenly he felt exhausted. He needed energy, food....

He opened his mouth and swallowed a cloud of cosmic dust. Bitter. He suddenly felt too hot. The nebula had now become a sac of anabiotic conservation which unbearably stuck to his skin. Something to wash himself with would come in handy. A jet of radiation for instance. Or, better, some ionised air. He felt the ions about him; already they seemed to emanate a strange astringency.

The stars around him exploded, making strange noises, static-like, at once acquiring shapes and shades. They were red in hue. The bright colour invaded him from everywhere bringing with it pain, a dull pain. This he sucked up voluptuously. He sucked up everything: heat, bitterness, redness, those crackling noises. At last the hunger disappeared. He could sleep now. Sleep. Just the glimpse of a thought followed by the illusion of plunging into deep lethargy. It was, however, the first thought that truly belonged to him. But there came another wish, linking to the first, breaking out unstoppably: movement. He was no longer everywhere: he was suspended in the abyss, condemned to a limited space by his own dimensions.

He tried to move. He could not. What was happening? A curious sensation. Sensation.... Yes, he was wide awake. And, therefore, alive. He must be still in the module. He was naked. The sensors adhering to his skin irritated him. The mask covering his mouth, nose, ears, eyes, that strange mask, was also uncomfortable. And he was not alone. He sensed there was someone there, beside him, watching him obsessively. He felt the need to move. He could not. He felt the need to control his body. He acquiesced, docilely, to the wishes of the other. Yes, he could breathe. He had been breathing through all this time. The air was strange, though. His heart was throbbing weakly in his ears, at its normal pace. His head ached. A bearable ache, pleasant even. He did not understand. Why should no movement be possible?

All of a sudden, Ted remembered that, in fact, he did not exist any longer. He must have died. The module cabin had crashed into the surface of the planet. Was he aboard the space shuttle by any chance? No: who would have carried him back there? He could not understand anything. It was as if he was living through some dreadful nightmare. Then, slowly, he became alert again. He could feel once more. The other was asking him to analyse himself, seemingly wanting to know if everything was all right with him. Who was he? How had this other managed to contact him? Just who *could* contact him? What was the meaning of it? He felt the need to scream, a refusal to accept a reality that could not be understood. The scream was there, in his chest, ready to break out.

He calmed down. How foolish he was. Was he able to communicate? Of course not, he was just able to feel and think. It was hot. He was surrounded by some sort of liquid. Could he feel his normal weight and still be immersed in a fluid? Why not, if this was another gravity? In that case, he could be neither on the shuttle nor on the space complex. He was lying on something solid. There was another environment that started from somewhere outside himself. He could neither see nor hear anything at all. Now he had no sensation of hunger or thirst; he was in complete comfort. Ted had never before experienced such a moment. There could be no such place in the galactic complex as this. There was no such place on the Earth either.... It was high time he controlled his thoughts. He had to get rid of the confusion that he felt.

He returned to his body. The warmth of the liquid invaded all of himself, even the right thigh and hip that had been grafted on him. That should have been impossible. He remembered perfectly that the artificial tissues implanted there were without a nerve system. They had given up trying to give them one because of the difficulty of integrating them with the rest of the neural network. This would have taken time. They had been in a hurry back then. Now he had nerves and a natural skin. He was complete again, exactly as before.

Ted's brain was working feverishly. The astronaut had no other choice but to accept two possibilities. First, he was in another space-time dimension, the subject of an intervention designed to regenerate his body which had been destroyed in an accident or to graft his head on another body. Second—he was on the planet onto which he had fallen so shamefully, the subject of an unimaginable intervention that had somehow brought him back to life.

He tried to remember. Through the thick fog of his thoughts he managed to see his solo departure on the reconnaissance flight meant to explore a double solar system. A system so strange for a double star. It was the first and probably the last more detailed exploration mission of that galaxy—a spherical space of almost fifty parsecs.

From the preliminary data of the ordinator he had chosen two planets—the third and the fourth. The only ones that belonged to the ecosphere presumed by the calculations. He had programmed the humanoid robot to explore the fourth planet, keeping the third for himself—it reminded him of the Earth. That had been his first mistake. He should not have separated from the robot.

He had put his own module into orbit around the planet and started investigating it, leaving the details to the instruments and the ordinator. There were two scarlet identical suns which never gave way to darkness, a gravity almost twice that of the Earth, highly fluctuating, thick clouds, and an atmosphere that would be highly aggressive to the living Earthly tissues. The temperature was bearable, and without significant variations. What had ever made him descend?

He seemed to have discovered water in its liquid state. He had then come across strange forms of life, in various stages of evolution. All the life-forms seemed to live by trapping light from the suns with the help of a greenish pigment. Ted remembered how close that was to the chlorophyll of the terrestrial vegetable kingdom. They could only be some sort of plant, then.

The strange vegetate forms ranged from the colonies of millions of micronic individuals to giant specimens hundreds of metres in width and height, on rigid skeletons of the silicon-carbon type. One of them was the size of a small Earthly bush and seemed to be moving, so he put it in a container meaning to take it to his spaceship. It looked as if it had somehow reacted to his presence there. There were more of the species in that place. They had been gathering around him, seemingly curious at his appearance. He was tempted to consider them forms of rudimentary intelligence, although no test proved conclusive.

The structure of the planet was not an uncommon

one. There were no mineral resources of interest. Life did not seem to have evolved into forms of superior intelligence. None of the instruments had detected any artificial energy fields. Everywhere the living structures disappeared near the poles giving way to rocky formations, a little more varied. These were probably volcanic in origin.

He was about to leave the orbit when he had detected that pulsating field. It was very weak and seemed to be generated by one of the poles. He decided to descend again, but not before sending to the Earth a small space vehicle with all his data and the container.

The decision to do that was his second mistake. The unpredictable field fluctuations and the engines struggling to handle them caused the disaster. Ted knew he could not survive the impact. Still, he found time to send a last message and harness the anti-grav generator of the module hoping for some miracle of survival. After that, there came nothingness....

Again he heard an inner voice which seemed, oddly enough, to have its origin on the outside. It was simply invading his thoughts, trying to reach him. At last Ted understood. His hunch turned into certainty. It was without doubt a telepathic message, outside of any spoken language. What was he supposed to do now? The one who had sent it was probably waiting for a similar response from him. Should he try to answer it? But how? He tried to focus. His head started to ache... ache...physical suffering.... No, he should try to change the tone of his brain activity in some way. The other would understand. He focused again.... No, that didn't work. He had to relax. Maybe to sleep. He knew he could do it, he had tried it before. But what if he would never wake up again? Fright clutched at his throat. He had to try. Slowly, self-suggestion calmed him down. He started the breathing cycles. He stopped thinking... nothing, nothing, nothing.

Yes! It had happened! He had violently been awakened by the other. The other knew Ted would understand. The other had decoded a message of physical discomfort then, more intensely, one of fear, and finally one of almost absolute quiet. The states through which Ted had passed were now being repeated in the same order. Full communication. The step had been taken.

* * * * * * *

The large Council Hall was bustling. All the heads of A and B priority departments of the entire intergalactic complex were there. Dan was there too. His tired face betrayed the fact that he had already taken the floor several times, letting himself be dissected by the sharp eyes of the others. The more aggressive ones had attacked him with their questions, asking for extra explanations. His proposals could not be put to the vote: it was obvious that he had lost the fight. His only hope lay in what he had said at the end of the debate. He had been allowed a last word and the councillors he relied on looked as if they may be willing to support him.

Olf had been watching the debate placidly, breaking

in rarely, emphasising ideas coming from both sides. Now the ball was in the court of the undecided. Suddenly, at the bottom of the big screen, appeared the recognition code of Ian, head of the complex security general department. He had been one of Dan's first opponents and he wanted to speak again.

Dan's reaction could hardly be noticed. These things were all the same to him. All the same, the next moment, with questioning eyes, he took off his earphones and turned his armchair towards Ian, waiting. He had to parry some new attack and could expect anything.

With a calm voice, persuasively, Ian began.

"Before we put an end to the debate, I'd like to draw your attention to the purpose of our colleague's research on Terra. I hope none of you'll object to this, will you?" He stopped, nodded contentedly, smiled and went on a little faster. "You all know how thorough our colleague claims to be when doing whatever research he does. This is regardless of the field: scientific, social, aesthetic, and so forth. Interdisciplinary research, to him, is an extremely vast phenomenon, which tends to control all branches of human activity or the main types of robots. And he uses this authoritarian attitude to control us and our ship and make us obey his will."

The murmur growing around him soon turned into a clamour that almost drowned his next words. The armchairs began a weird dance while the astronauts were shouting confusedly. Dan stayed calm, fixing the speaker as if trying to skewer him with his eyes. The latter was fully enjoying the effect of his speech. After a while he stretched out his arms, hands open, in a defensive gesture, and said.

"I know, these are serious charges, but I must ask you to listen and then decide for yourselves."

The hubbub faded away. Ian knew now that no one would stop him. Even his enemies were preparing to listen. They were more tense than ever.

"Let's return to Terra then. I've got here a list of all the education centres in which Dan has delivered some very interesting lectures."

Ian's image on the screen got smaller and gave way to a piece of paper on which someone had written something. It was clearly a hurried scrawl. After a minute of silence, he went on.

"Our colleague has, among other things, put forward a few thoughts about the phenomenology of human knowledge. A little philosopher, you might say. Nothing to wonder about. Trans-disciplinary research is itself a kind of philosophic concept. And what's the essence of this concept? The great experts are just a bunch of narrow-minded people, lacking all perspective, turned towards themselves and not to the outside world. Therefore, the world will have to belong to and be led by those who, as our colleague once put it himself, know less and less about more and more things. With a mere quip he overrules us all. He denies your competence as leaders of the services and levels you run. He, however, represents the new system which will put things in order, with everyone in their place. And he will be the number one, of course—the absolute decision-maker. Look here," said Ian and pointed to a paragraph in red on the screen, "see how he assures us that the greatest specialists in the narrowest of fields will have to be replaced—inevitably—by AI expert programs. And look here," he pointed to another paragraph, "see how he thinks researchers will have to give up their studies in depth to go back to creation, comprehensive views, general directions, and philosophy. And here, see how he accuses us of bending over our desks dissecting and furnishing data to the huge biotronic brains that establish inter-connections and link disparate events in man's activity in order to generalise and postulate laws and directions of evolution. They thus assure themselves of their supremacy over us. Old ideas and attitudes adapted speculatively to sound like real facts. Simple and effective! Listen! I'm not finished yet!" shouted Ian above the hubbub of the room. "I want to give you the evidence that incriminates him."

His eyes flashed as if he were possessed while his arms were trying to calm down the audience. He went on, still almost shouting.

"Dan claims philosophy, in its current stage, is at a dead end. He says the discovery of the mysteries of the universe are way ahead of it, providing it with data which it itself should have provided. He also says that, in the past, there were moments when people could see things clearly, making a neat distinction between knowledge, its objects and its means, managing, through a philosophic concept, to smoothen the way for science, to guide it, and foresee a discovery. Today the situation's exactly the other way round and Dan finds it more than normal."

While the rest of the audience was listening intently, Dan kept to his seat, immobile, his eyes half-closed in an obvious attempt at self-control.

"Well, he, the adept of inter-disciplinarity as he sees it, cannot be but a philosopher of genius. He is able, knowing so little about so many things, to create his own philosophic system," said Ian mockingly. "Very well then, he is neither the first nor the last to try it. Look, however, at how important he thinks the idea of the structural informatisation of the Universe."

Two more pages full of texts and diagrams appeared on the screen.

"Here's the recrudescence of some millennium-old theories. They were once given up because of their purely speculative nature, and are now launched again by a bunch of people whose authority has not been recognised officially. And what are these people up to, may I ask?"

For several minutes there was no reaction coming from the audience. Most of them watched the screen silently, only a few trying to make some notes.

"Now look at Dan's plan, look at how he wants to put his theories into practice, how he tries to change the program of the galactic complex. If you can imagine that, re-organise the whole Universe. Dan," continued Ian, his voice now hollow and threatening, "in the presence of the Council I accuse you of attempting to hijack the space program, to take control of the crew and make them serve your personal purposes. I also accuse you of deliberately misinforming the Council and the crew and undermining the authority and leadership of the other chiefs. Your ambition has absolutely no limits. You must be prevented from infecting the astronauts with your dangerous ideas. And that can be done only by your excommunication."

Exhausted by his oratorical effort, Ian collapsed into his armchair while the deep silence around him gave the impression of a vacuum capable of unleashing a devastating implosion. Nothing happened, however. With easy, well-controlled movements, Dan switched the picture and sound captor on himself.

"You've listened to Ian's speech with an attention that, under different circumstances, I'd have found most flattering. It was a remarkable speech in its own way, indeed, and I can't help envying Ian for that. The trouble is it sounded like an indictment of what were simply my well-meant proposals. They were skilfully and—why not—slyly distorted to the benefit of himself and our captain. For it was undoubtedly our captain Olf that influenced his speech so effectively. It was so easy for everyone to see the unmistakable features of the captain's handwriting on the big screen. I for one can't understand this rudimentary mistake. It was the result of haste, no doubt, made during this meeting. Olf probably felt the need to break in and did so, with some success, I must admit that. But why through Ian?"

Dan's enquiring eyes serenely swept the flabbergasted audience, stopping at the other end of the room where Olf was sitting with his face to the wall. As if he felt he was being watched, the captain jumped to his feet, turned and burst out:

"I declare the meeting closed. I give Dan forty-eight hours to come up with definite arguments in support of his program. The ones presented here are not sufficiently acceptable. Ian's proposal stays open."

With quick jerky movements, Olf made his way through the audience and left the hall.

* * * * * * *

For once Eva was not in her activity area. She was in the relaxation room watching the Council meeting on the video-monitor. She had not missed a thing. She was out of breath, her mind a tumble of grim thoughts and contradictions.

The harsh dispute in the Council Hall was the result of a long sequence of disagreements that had seemed to take them nowhere. Because of these arguments the ship had passed through great dangers. They had detected intelligent extraterrestrial life and many of the astronauts had wanted to stop and examine the area. Then the crew split into two, one side building a new ship and trying but failing to make the contact. At the time they had been able to save the expedition, the biotronic ordinator had still been active and efficient. Now, however, they were alone, and the others' experience was so far away. Now it was not just the potential contact that they could make; now they had the chance to unravel a mystery which involved the failure of an expedition and, above all, Ted's disappearance.

Eva could not decide whether to see the disactivation of the huge computer as a positive or a negative factor. She only knew that the crew had been left alone with their own problems of conscience and action. They would be without the cold impartial arbitration of that brain that somehow represented the ship itself. She knew that Ted had disappeared in the immensity of the Universe and that, all of a sudden, there were hopes of his retrieval. Yet these seemed to involve a gamble with not only his own life but also that of another, completely unknown. Did they have the right to take such risks? Weren't Dan's plans crazy enough to compromise the expedition? How far could the struggle between fear and human solidarity, the wish to know, go? How responsible was she for this? As though he had understood her, little Tim gave up playing with the magnetic spheres, looked wonderingly at the video-monitor for a moment, then slipped into her arms, staring at her with his big eyes full of candour.

"Mummy! Mummy, what's excommunication?"

That was too much for Eva who burst into tears hugging Tim in despair.

"Oh, Ted, my dear Ted!" she murmured through her tears.

That is how Mag found her. She stared at her for quite a while, then turned to the door where Dan was waiting, his face devoid of all expression.

"We are with you, Dan...to the bitter end," she said,

with a twinkle in her deep, impenetrable eyes.

* * * * * * *

The Communion Hall was full. More than five thousand Varyans had climbed up through the access tubes from the basements and blocked their soles obediently in expectation of the great event. From the central trap-door, the crowd of antennae moving in a disorderly way gave the impression of a bizarre dance, not to music but to the whistles of the greenish creatures that were showing their excitement. They were about to see and feel the Bearer of the Great Spirit, of the very essence of existence on Var.

Given the importance of the event, there were present only the leaders who had not contacted Him yet. There were few of them to have seen Him twice. They were about to share Pure Knowledge, the Great Revelation. Only He was the bearer of the message.

Below, in the basements of the Hall, several technicians were carefully fixing upon the greenish cylinder of the Professor's body the last accessories of the field zoom. These were mounted discreetly behind the antennae. They were covering everything but the antennae, the mouth, and the eyes with a bright fabric. The limbs' suckers were free to move, ready to handle the controls of the apparatus. At last they placed him on the trap which carried him slowly to the middle of the Communion Hall.

His appearance was welcomed with an excited whistling from the massed assembly which ended abruptly when the trap stopped. In the heavy silence hundreds of thousands of antennae turned towards one point.

"I am the Bearer of the Great Spirit—the essence of knowledge. I am the bearer of the message of He who created and will destroy this world; He to whom you owe your existence as superior beings. I am the Bearer of Pure Reason, the Meaning of the Entire World. I am the Owner of Absolute Truth," murmured the Professor watching the effect of his words on the audience, and slightly turned the switch of the installation.

The bodies of the thousands of Varyans started to tremble. One by one, their soles slipped sideways leaving the rest of the bodies in unlikely suspension, with the suckers draped across their small mouths as if trying to stifle a shout. After a while they could hardly hear the click behind the Professor as they collapsed on the floor.

* * * * * * *

"You've overdone it," said Orm to the Professor. "They'll surely need some time to recover."

They were behind the building in one of the most isolated departments of the Institute.

"It doesn't matter. They must know well the kind of force that rules them. Now tell me quickly what happened in Lab 5. Where's Sit?"

"I left him there. I had to have him take the test of truth. We could lose control of the situation at any time."

"How come?" shouted the Professor and his soles

started to clatter on the slabs while his limbs were pointing their suckers at Orm. It was as if they were trying to wrap him up. "Did you forget what you had to do? What's going on?"

"As a member of the group that is at the Pole, Sit's already made some experiments in biofield focusing. I'm sure the southerners are more advanced than we are in such techniques. Here, apart from the installation you've just used and the one in Lab 5, there's nothing else. And don't forget he's built them both...."

"You'll have to wrest those secrets from him."

"I don't know if I'll be able to. The volition annihilator can't be used too often without affecting the intellect. Sit's managed to reintegrate the cosmic being in the biofield specially created for it. I attended the experiment myself. Can you imagine the consequences of a contact? Do you realise the creature's rational? It even seems to belong to a civilisation that's more powerful and more advanced than ours. Where are the other creatures similar to it? Where do they come from? What are they up to?"

The Professor reacted violently. His psyche got blocked. His antennae, flabby now, fell along his contorting body, adhering to it as if trying to prevent it from collapsing. He was about to fall when, at Orm's sign, two giant Varyans rushed up to him and carried him to the revitalisation room. There, optical systems focused an intense pulsing flux of sunrays coming from the outside.

"Take good care of him," Orm ordered the two

Varyans who were taking the Professor's clothes off. "Don't leave the room until he's recovered. Meanwhile you can expose yourselves to a little of the light, too."

"Thank you, Master," the giants shouted gratefully plunging into the stream of light and uttering grotesque whistles.

* * * * * * *

While handling the power installations of the laboratory, Sit assessed his chances. He had just changed the characteristics of the annihilator. That could help in case he had to use it on himself a second time. Then it would be important for him to make himself indispensable here so that they would not remove him. It would be great if he managed to achieve the contact between the Trills and the Varyans. He had managed to make just one exchange of information with the monster using the Trills' biological flux, but was that all that he could do?

Sit was somehow at his wits' end. This creature had something that the Varyans lacked. On the other hand, these Trills puzzled him more than ever. Were they intelligent or not? Wasn't he wrong in thinking they were inferior creatures? What if that was the exclusive merit of the terminal? A Varyan did not have access to the fundamental matrix of a Trill, this amazing creature that could communicate through a biofield and resonate with the biofluxes of another Trill or even those of the extra-Varyan. Thus it achieved a transfer of information that defied time and any distance.

Why couldn't he, Sit, use those codes he had partially deciphered in the monster? Did he have only to shape and structure them between certain limits?

But then he really felt he was the owner of one of the great secrets of the Universe. He had the key to a certain form of manifestation of highly organised matter. He knew how to handle an information mechanism of unprecedented dimensions. For the fist time he was sure of the minority technocratic group at the other pole of the planet. The triumph of intelligence over force and obscurantism was near.

Six generations of technocratic Varyans had been working on a phenomenon which was now being experimented for the first time on a rational creature coming from the infinite of the Universe. The experiment was about to fully succeed. Pushing the button to resume contact, Sit looked at Ted through the transparent walls. He found the creature fascinating. He had reconstructed it, given it life and now he was sending it messages. Was it going to understand them?

* * * * * * *

With her first steps on the access passage to the research department, Eva heaved a sigh of relief. The pale blue colour of the walls, broken regularly by the programmers of micro-climatisation installations, had a beneficial effect on the woman. Her steps aroused before her waves of light that flowed generously from the ceiling. Now and then these turned into a restful white.

For one thing, the time spent under the big cupola of the recovery level had been a total waste. She had come across an Earthly winter program. Trembling even in her fur-lined mantle, she had sat for a while on an old tree trunk placed cleverly across the banks of a half-frozen stream, buried in the overpowering white snow. Giving up the idea of having a walk, she had assessed, half-amused, the decorators' efforts to create a feeble tree on the other bank of the stream, behind a pile of stones. The branches of this glimmered silently and coldly, reflecting the artificial sunlight. The setting, far from being comforting, looked nostalgic and oppressive, suggesting the hostility of the cold dark vacuum they were crossing rather than the illusion of the planet they had left for such a long time.

But Eva belonged to the stars, like many other astronauts in that complex. She was born in space, despite the deep-rooted custom of the young mothers to give birth to their babies on their native planet. Maybe that was why these Earthly sights seemed less impressive. The pale blue colour, characteristic of all the information processing centres created by man on the Earth or any spatial complex, was much more familiar to her.

Tim was also a child of the stars, as she had always wanted. Tim, Tim, Tim, the waves of light and the undulating melodic lines coming from the walls kept echoing her thoughts. Suddenly she recognised a tune of the environmental creation department where she had first met Ted. The melodic lines touched her ears, syncopatedly, in tune with her steps and the waves of light: Ted, Ted, Ted, they seemed to say, and Eva found herself smiling. She had at last the chance to do something for Tim and Ted, to try and find her husband. He had to be alive.

She did not care about breaking the rules. She was going to get into the command centre of the research department, where only the captain and the level chiefs were authorised to enter. She alone was going to master the entire ordinator, second in importance only to the biotronic brain. Dan had explained to her how to deal with it.... How could Dan have so much confidence in her? And Mag....

On seeing the dark blue door, she started and tightened under her arm the bag of data with which Mag had hurriedly provided her. She slowed down, then stopped, her legs fixed on the floor by the lead that seemed to be trickling through her veins. Instinctively, her hand went down to her belt and fully activated one of the programmers. Almost immediately she felt her earlobes and fingers warm up, while a wave of ice overcame her soles mounting through her hips like a shower of ionised air able to change her entire body into a feather. All these sensations blended into a feeling of calm and security. Then she was lucid again, in full control of her thoughts and reflexes.

She glanced over her shoulder. The passage was empty. With a quick and precise movement she took from her left sleeve pocket a small matt-grey card and put it in the console on the access door, as Dan had shown her. Then she stepped back, waiting. If she was caught red-handed, she could thwart the whole plan conceived by Dan and Mag a few hours ago. For Dan in particular lending his ID card would mean total disgrace. He had risked a great deal now that he was being watched by Ian's men.

Eva had never before broken the rules that had been devised by all the members of the expedition. The few cases of insubordination had appeared involuntarily, as a consequence of carelessness or as "cases of emergency," as Ian had strangely put it. But Dan had said their action might also be called that if they could prove it. Dan and Mag...why had they got involved in this? Not only because of Ted, she was sure of that.

After moments that seemed an eternity, the door slid quietly aside, leaving a narrow opening in the wall through which came a streak of light. Eva stepped in, looked for the button to shut the door. Only after the diffusedly lit ceiling of the passage disappeared did she lean lightly against the wall and sigh with relief.

* * * * * * *

Mag had a look at the screen on her bracelet and started. She was running out of time. She began to uncouple the installations in a hurry which betrayed her tiredness. The features of her strangely beautiful, almost unreal face were stern now pointing to the fight between physical exhaustion and stubborn will.

For almost a whole day, Mag had been in a ceaseless clash with time and the difficulties of a complex program. Now, however, she had to go. Eva was waiting for her in the research department. The wish to find her husband had worked miracles with her friend. But what about her? What was it that was driving her on? The remains of her affection for Ted? Her sympathy for Eva and her son, Tim? Her self-pride stimulated by an exceptional situation in which she could show her competence? The research of a phenomenon whose secrets she had always wanted to reveal? The answer could be any of these things. Anyway, she did know she was part of an action initiated by Dan. This could be decisive for him, Ted, Eva, Tim, and maybe for the whole spaceship.

Her thoughts raced involuntarily towards Dan. The man's face appeared before her with astonishing clarity. She smiled—her subconscious had reconstructed his face quite often lately.... The truth was that yesterday's meeting had been a revelation for her. Dan was indeed very special. Did he mean more to her than she was ready to admit? The distance she had kept between her and the men on the ship since Ted and she had been a couple was turning against her. Her unshakeable will, her affective independence were yielding, giving way to a powerful emotion. Funny, she said to herself, Dan did not seem to have ever been interested in a woman. Not on the complex, and not before that.

She looked at the reflecting panels next to her. No, she could not appear like this in front of him. Then, hesitatingly, she took a small silvery tube and coupled it to her belt, in a place specially made for it. Mag had never used this before.

* * * * * * *

Eva was exultant. Everything was going to plan. The installations in front of her were extremely unusual but not because of their complexity; quite the contrary, they looked like a game for children. Their simplicity was disarming. Later on, when she found everything she needed to start work, she realised this command centre had been devised for non-computer scientists.

While she was pressing the keys, seeing out of the corner of her eye the data displayed on the screens, it crossed her mind that she had never met such a discrepancy between the potential of the installations and the form they had been given. For their potential was indeed amazing. An immense joy flooded her at the thought that soon she and this ordinator would make up a single will. She felt like an artist in the fever of creation, who had just acquired a tool bordering on perfection. With a roguish smile in the corner of her mouth she started to outline the auxiliary programs.

* * * * * * *

Before leaving the laboratory, Mag looked again at the quartz globe under which was pulsating the creature retrieved from the container sent by Ted, before he died. The changes in its morphology and energy consumption had appeared at the same time as Tim's weird dreams. Everything had started from there. Still, there was one thing that Mag had never mentioned to Dan—it was so extraordinary. The pulsating creature had slowly taken on the form of a human brain. Beyond the mixture of repulsion and fascination she felt for that thing, an idea for which she was going to fight with all her strength was beginning to take shape: changing the program of the expedition. They had to go back....

* * * * * * *

How long had she been here? For an eternity, it seemed. Exhaustion was tearing her away from reality. Before the door Eva was standing still, holding in her right hand the code-carrying card. She breathed hard, trying to calm herself. She looked at the bracelet on her wrist the same way that Mag did it, and at just the same time in the space biology laboratory.

"If only they came sooner," she murmured as if to herself.

Dan was waiting for the reports on Level B. They certainly had a lot to talk about. In her left hand Eva was holding the package of information she had taken out of the computer until she made the mistake. But was it a mistake? Undoubtedly.

Something told her that only her love for Ted was to blame. She did not feel guilty at all. She had indeed started to hope Ted was still alive. At first it had seemed impossible, crazy, but now the situation was different. The computer's reaction was too unusual for such a banal conclusion as the one that the leaders of the spaceship had come to a year ago.

Eva could remember everything in the smallest

detail. Ted's last message before his fall was very clear. The film recording of the catastrophe, made by the watch and control spaceship system, was as clear as her memory. The robot had processed the data by itself and ordered the ship to return to the second module on the neighbouring planet, and from there to go on to the orbital complex. No other signal had been received from the devices embedded in the astronaut's suit.

Eva had not managed to convince the Council members to send another shuttle there. The mission had been accomplished, the distance was too big for a shuttle anyway. Everything was known except for the reason why Ted had returned to the planet. Dan had pleaded so much during yesterday's meeting for unravelling the mystery of that expedition. There was, however, nothing to be found in the recordings. Everything was obvious: they had lost an explorer and a module and it was only his own fault. They did not want to risk such losses again. Planets with gravity anomalies could not be explored without hazard. They could do no more than try to retrieve Ted's body, if there was still anything left to be retrieved. In the end Eva had given in. She was left with Tim, her only comfort.

Everything had started with Tim. The child was more than four years old at that time and he could recount his dreams clearly. A year after the catastrophe he began asking for his father. He could see him, he felt he was alive.... What sort of a strange creature did Mag keep in her laboratory? Eva had not seen it yet but the computer said a great deal about it....

The computer invaded Eva's thoughts again, reminding her of the terrible thing she had done almost deliberately there. Yes, it was better for no one to get in. Quickly she pressed the keys on the door console to block access completely, withdrew Dan's ID card, and left the passage in a hurry.

* * * * * * *

Sit put the encoded message to Ted in the incinerator. It had been a long message and the Varyan had no idea how much of it the creature before him had received. He knew it by heart, he had tried hard to express it properly. The message was full of information about Var and the Varyans, how they had both come to be here, in this laboratory. A common destiny united them—confronting the members of the Institute who wanted to destroy the extra-Varyan in order to analyse him, and to destroy Sit because he was not one of them.

Despite the fact that he was sleeping, Ted did receive the signal. The telepathic contact made him go back to his senses. The Varyan seemed eager to resume communication. He was hurriedly telling him something about the planet which he called Var. He was telling him about the reconstruction of his body that had taken the members of the Institute a lot of tests and observations of his biological codes.

On Var, Ted learned, all beings lived by processing the radiations of the two suns which they converted into chemical energy. The only mobile species were the Varyans and some inferior beings called Trills that lived on the surface of the planet. To those Trills did Ted owe his life as they could create, shape, and copy a biofield. By a unique chance, on his first descent a group of Trills had contacted Ted and copied the matrix of his biological code. Then he had been brought to this Institute where Sit was the only one to have access to the secrets of living matter.

By capturing the Trills that had contacted Ted, Sit obtained the key to the modulation of the field that brought the astronaut back to life. It was that field that was operating now, facilitating the contact between them by a transfer of information at the basic, primary level.

The Varyans were probably descended from the Trills. These Trills were very mobile and had several antennae by means of which they fed on electromagnetic energy. Unlike the Trills, the Varyans lived inside the planet and captured photons only to find their way around. They exposed their skin to the sun partly for pleasure and partly for re-balancing their metabolism.

At first, the Varyans communicated among themselves by their bioenergy fields. Later, when they lost that skill, they developed a means of communication based on written signs which marked the beginning of their current civilisation. They started to shape the underground and to make good use of its elements. At the same time they focused on manoeuvring matter at its structural level.

The information that Ted was receiving was too

much for him. He found it harder and harder to understand it. His cerebral cortex was getting inhibited, denying access to the telepathic fluxes. He felt his head was being seized by a merciless fire, ready to burn him up. Between one fit of unbearable pain and another he managed to learn something about some open conflicts and the partition of the planet into two zones of influence; he, Sit, was a technocratic analyst who had been infiltrated with scientists of the North and there was danger of his being found out.... All this information was too much for Ted's brain, and made it refuse to perceive anything else. With a last scream his nerves gave in and Ted lost consciousness.

Sit did not hear the click of the door mechanism. He looked completely absorbed in the flimsy bands spread across his limbs like a fan. They were the bearers of the latest messages sent through the biofield to the container where the extra-Varyan was. The blocked lock made a slight noise again and this time Sit heard it. The Varyan moved his antennae in alarm. He went to the wall quickly and began to touch it with his antennae eager not to miss any vibration. He slowly reached the access-trap and his antennae stopped rustling around the lock and stuck hard to the metal.

The noises he perceived from the other side troubled him. His big eyes surveyed the entire laboratory, then stopped and stared at a large trolley full of apparatus nearby. The Varyan pushed it with his soles against the access-trap. He was just in time. A big boom shook the building and the metal door split. A second later the alarm was set off. Sit heard the thuds, more frequent and more violent now. He saw with horror how the access-trap yielded, its surface getting covered by dozens of cracks snaking from the lock towards the hinges.

Almost hypnotised by that web of fissures, Sit tried to weigh his chances. He had to destroy the recordings. In the rhythmic vibrations of the walls and the floor, he rushed to the incinerator but, remembering that burning the recordings might take too much time, he changed his mind. Whistling spitefully, he went straight to the annex workshop which had a long grey tube in its midst. He climbed up the installation, set it off, and directed the tube to the floor.

The first piece of the trap flew away at the same time that the intense beam of luminous radiations gusted from the tube. Clumsily, Sit swept the bands, colouring them in brilliant silver. The breaches in the access-trap got bigger revealing the feverish activity outside. The researcher must have been noticed because for some moments there were no blows. The pause was more than welcome for Sit who thus was able to finish his destruction of the recordings.

The scientist then turned to the desk trying to change the characteristics of the luminous flux. The direction of the tube, aiming at the access-trap, left no doubts about his intentions. He did not have the time, though. A powerful explosion pulverised the rest of the access-trap as well as the improvised barricade. The blast hurled the scientist against the opposite wall.

Through the gaping hole almost immediately a group of Varyans rushed in, urged on by Orm's hurried whistles. For a moment, Sit and Orm stared at each other, then unexpectedly the former jumped to the installations. The distance between him and the aggressors seemed to give him another chance. But he heard Orm shout.

"Now!"

Two huge soldiers appeared before him and, with incredibly quick movements, used their suckers to tear out pieces from their own bodies. Then their limbs began to launch the strange projectiles at Sit and the installation. Sit found himself blocked by the organic gelatinous rain. The flabby bits from the aggressors' bodies stuck with a dry snap onto the scientist, covering his eyes, his antennae, his limbs, immobilising him completely. Seized with impotent fury, the Varyan tried hopelessly to free himself but he finally fell down, fixed to the floor by the shapeless green mass that now covered him entirely. The two giants rushed to their victim whistling triumphantly. They threw themselves against Sit, pressing him and covering him with their bodies and limbs.

Through the curtain of choking smoke that filled the room, Orm could hardly see what was happening. Whistling sharply, he finally dashed after the two soldiers who were already merging with the moving matter they had covered. At the last moment, Orm drew a long rod from under his mantle and launched on the two clusters of antennae a yellowish dust that stiffened them almost instantaneously. At the same speed a sucker coming from behind blocked the rod and Orm found himself shoved aside. Angrily, he turned around ready to fight but changed his mind when he saw the Professor.

"Why did you do that? His flesh was their reward. They deserved it," the Professor said looking impassively at the soldiers' agonised movements.

"I need him alive, understand? Alive!" Orm burst out and threw the weapon away. "They were my guards. I cared for them.... One moment of carelessness and...," Orm said staring at the immobile mass in front of him. "An enemy, a southerner, a damned southerner, whom we still need...."

Then Orm turned and whistled nervously at the assault troops who were standing stiff, watching the scene in silence.

"Take the one that's alive out! Move! Faster, faster!"

Hesitatingly, the soldiers complied with the order, then began to clean up Sit's body with their suckers covered by protective sacs. Finally, they used a portable projector to send a powerful flux of electromagnetic field over his antennae. After a while, the scientist showed signs of life. His eyelids shook spasmodically, then he opened his eyes and looked confusedly in all directions. Before he recovered completely, questions rushed upon him with the force of a bewildering blow.

"Have you contacted the monster?"

"Who's he?"

"Where does he come from?"

"How long's he going to live like that?"

"Where're his fellow creatures?"

"Have you contacted the extremists?"

"What's the state of your biofield researches?"

"What're your plans?"

"Who're you collaborating with?"

Sit answered monosyllabically, unevenly, interrupted by convulsions of his body that almost made him jump in the air. At last, with a desperate whistle, he managed to wave to one of the desks on which they could see a pile of hurriedly written papers.

"It's the report I asked him for!" exclaimed Orm and went up to the desk while Sit's torture ended in a continuous tremor.

"Leave him alone!" the Professor broke in. "His body's given in. He won't recover too soon."

He went to the other end of the laboratory where Ted was lying as usual. After examining the Earthling carefully through the transparent wall and liquid, he moved away and, looking around, whistled authoritatively.

"Prepare the troops to be deployed. No technocrat shall survive the final operation. Half the troops shall go up to the surface. I want them to exterminate the Trills. No Trill shall be left alive on this planet. As for that creature," the Professor pointed some of his antennae to Ted, "it consumes too much energy. I want the force installations to be well guarded. I will have the creature transferred to my own laboratory where I will analyse it myself."

The Professor turned around on one of his soles and hurried out followed closely by all. Once again, Sit remained alone with the Earthling, lying unconsciously on the slabs of the room.

* * * * * *

When the two women entered the room, Dan stood up and looked at them enquiringly.

"I've been expecting you," he said, a feverish glow in his eyes.

"You've been expecting us or the results of our investigations?" Mag's voice tried in vain to sound light-hearted.

After a moment of hesitation, the man said:

"We must hurry. Is everything OK?"

"Eva's got the papers."

"Show them to me. Time's against us."

Eva handed him a pile of papers then let herself fall into an armchair. In a strange silence, the astronaut looked over the notes most carefully. After a while he looked up and stared at Eva questioningly.

"You've got it right. The report isn't finished," she said.

"Something prevented her from getting all the information," Mag added. "I suggest we put everything we know together. Once we've had a general picture, we'll be able to...."

Dan did not answer right away. He considered it and said, frowning.

"OK, I'm listening."

"This creature," Mag said, "is structurally unique. It doesn't seem to be the result of natural evolution, although...when it comes to its exchanges with the environment, it is quite similar to terrestrial metabolisms."

"What do you mean? Does it have reactions characteristic of a dissipating structure?"

"I have detected negative entropic processes which are, however, controlled by something other than an informational program comprised in its internal organisation.... But I haven't found any genetic codes."

"Do you think it couldn't have something like that?" asked Dan wonderingly.

"Not quite.... Anyway, the process of growth and multiplication moves in mysterious ways which don't seem to be linked to the structure of the plant."

"Wait a minute. Did you say 'plant'? Why?"

"Although it's superior in mobility to our vegetation, it did not show any desire to move."

Dan looked at her puzzled.

"Didn't it react in any way?"

Mag found it hard to answer.

"It stays in the environment I've created for it and absorbs radiations from almost the entire spectrum. Even gamma radiations. Without a photo I couldn't make out its structure. It's more impenetrable than a heavy alloy."

"Its structure," Eva broke in, "is a mixture of carbon and silicon. Carbon shows in metabolic exchanges, while silicon's present in sub-structures, as its compounds are more stable and unsuitable for energy reactions."

"But how come the structure of this plant—if you want to call it that—is chemically inert?" Dan asked. "It's obvious the creature's defending itself by annihilating all lab interventions. Asking it to give us its attention won't solve anything. It must be forced to react. We're running out of time!"

"Just let me go on," said Mag in a slightly conciliatory tone. "You're right, such an approach will take us nowhere. There's something else that puzzles me, though. This creature's changed morphologically by itself. It's increased its size, and taken the shape of a human brain—only it's dull green in colour. And it's absorbed too much energy."

"All these changes must be its reaction to the outside world," Dan said. "It's almost impossible to link them to the telepathic phenomena we've witnessed." He looked at the two women as if expecting them to contradict him.

Eva turned her head slightly and said, a little embarrassed.

"The computer said telepathic phenomena are the result of a possible energy field existing everywhere in the Universe. It also said the plant's contacted something from the outside."

"Strange," Dan said thoughtfully. "What else did it say?"

"It seems," Eva went on more confidently, "that these phenomena of negative entropy, as Mag calls them, can interact with this field depending on their structural and informational characteristics."

"The human brain doesn't create any kind of waves, on the contrary it uses the field to send or receive information at a primary or more evolved level, according to its ability to modulate it," Mag added.

"The computer said there's a source of information that's feeding the creature in the lab," Eva said.

"On the planet it comes from?" Dan winced as if lashed.

"Why not? Maybe Ted himself...," Eva whispered.

The astronaut forced himself to smile.

"Do you think there may be an interaction between Ted and the creature?" Dan started to stride around the room. "The creature *must* have contacted something. Its current shape seems to be a signal for us.... But what's more important now is the processing of this information here, on our spaceship."

"This plant, or animal," Eva said in a more neutral voice, "has the unusual skill to store and send information to beings it gives birth to by self-division. That's why we haven't been able to find a genetic program. There's no need for it. Every being carries in itself its own field in which one can find all the information necessary for survival and reproduction."

"What happens to this field when the being dies?" Dan asked.

"It could be completely transferred to other beings. They send information to one another, modulating with their structures the lines of the primordial field.

These lines can be perceived and decoded by the other beings," Eva answered.

"It's as if a group of people communicated among themselves just by telepathy and moved only by telekinesis," Mag said, staring at the ceiling.

"Could such a group evolve?" Dan asked.

"It depends on the amount of information such a structure can store," Eva replied.

"Then," Dan concluded, "an extraterrestrial being copies Ted's image, memorises it, and sends it to Tim a year after Ted's death. Then it changes its shape so as to look exactly the same as the organ that can receive information here. That Tim is the receiver doesn't strike me as odd at all, because he is Ted's child. I know that in such cases one's nearest relatives are always preferred. But why now?"

"You're wrong," Mag said. "You've forgotten the ordinator presupposes the existence of an information source on that planet, not on our ship. The creature's apparently acting only as a transmission relay."

"And you really think Ted's there? He's been dead for a year and now he's risen and is sending information? No way. It's ridiculous," Dan said.

"Wrong again," Eva broke in. "I thought that too until I fed it into the computer."

"So?"

"The computer asked me if Tim had been conceived in this galaxy."

"And?"

"I said yes. Then the computer went mad."

"You must be joking," Dan said earnestly. "A computer can't go mad."

"No, it can't," Eva laughed. "It's just a way of putting it."

"Was it a joke then?" Mag asked and looked at her in surprise.

"Half a joke. The ordinator asked me to cancel all the answers it had given before that moment."

"What?!"

"It asked me to consider them invalid. Then the overload alarm signals set off. I asked it what was going on. And what do you think it did? It asked me to connect it to the central information stock through the central brain of the ship."

"The biotronic brain," Mag murmured, her face turned to stone.

"I knew the capacity of the machine would increase by that so I did it," Eva said.

"But that's not possible without the captain's approval," said Dan taken aback.

"Do you realise what would've happened if I'd contacted Olf? Normally, it wouldn't have been a problem, but under the circumstances.... Anyway, everything happened so fast," said Eva and stopped. Her breathing had got faster. The woman was living again the moments that had disturbed her so much in the past few hours. The small beads of sweat on her forehead made her fixed gaze stand out. "The ordinator realised the operation was illegal and fooled me. It asked me to connect it to the self-security device. That device doesn't allow any outsider or outside program to disconnect the ordinator from the central memory. Only the biotronic brain can do it."

Eva grimaced with fright and despair at the memory of those moments. She went on, her voice strangled with emotion.

"I don't know why I made that mistake. The fatigue, the fear that the program might fail, the thought that Ted might be alive, everything came over me at that moment."

"What did you do? Did you connect it?" The man's voice sounded more worried than ever before.

Mag kept her eyes closed as if not thinking of anything.

"You connected it, didn't you?" This time Dan did not expect any answer. "The biotronic brain wasn't disconnected. Such a thing is impossible, it has its own sources of energy. However, the Council's decided to block all its actions. It's cancelled its right to run the ship, to supervise all departments, to keep itself informed. It's like a paralysed giant who's been left with only the right to think. You've just connected it to a classical ordinator, with terminals, interface equipment, optical circuits of the basic modules and all— that is with a nose, a mouth, with eyes, and ears, and a few fingers. How many operational robots serve the research computer?"

"Two of them are active. The others have been neutralised. I managed to annihilate those by blocking the control codes. I couldn't reach those two, though.

They told me they'd been instructed to keep working and to prevent their disconnection. It was a real nightmare, being alone with all those machines which suddenly seemed to obey me only when they wanted to. It was terrible...."

"Two fingers, then," Dan concluded. "Not very many. What class are they?"

"One's a gamma—good at everything—just a doer. But the other's an alpha, a little ordinator on wheels. It normally does research work. The former seems quite dangerous, though. It's very mobile and skilful."

"They're not humanoids," Mag added. "They haven't got programs for ordinary relations with people. The first law of robotics is quite simple with them, easy to counteract through clever orders."

Dan began to stride around the room again, trying to control his agitation by massaging his temples.

"They must be destroyed. Through them the biotronic brain can control the ship—not on a large scale—but it can do it. Eva, perhaps we should warn the security corps, and do that as soon as we can. Tell me, how did the ordinator react after being connected?"

"It thanked me. In fact, that was when I realised I'd lost control of it. I tried to cut off its energy supply, but it branched almost at once to the autonomous units of the brain. Then it asked me to let it access Mag's lab saying it was very important to it to research the being from the third planet in the KH-09 solar system. Then I turned it down, then...there was no more then. It stopped speaking to me, insensitive to all my calls."

"And now, what's it doing?" Mag asked.

"It must be doing the internal programs received from the central unit. The optotronic brain is active again."

"It's always been active, don't forget that!" Dan said. "Lacking memory and not able to communicate, it was almost non-existent for us. It can't influence the other terminals, anyway. If we close down the computer research department, we'll isolate it again."

"I've blocked the access door, but I'm afraid an indirect action on the ship is still possible. Through the central data unit it runs, the biotronic brain can poison all the level computers. We'll have to tell them all to confine themselves to their own memories."

Eva was gradually yielding to emotion and fatigue, her face buried in her hands. In the growing silence of the room her breathing got deeper and more even. She fell asleep, her blond hair overflowing the armchair, her face relaxed and young again, refusing the burden of the past hours.

"What shall we do now?" Mag whispered after a long while, looking into the man's eyes.

Dan turned towards a panel and reached for the alarm key of the security department.

"Dan, you know too well you won't have a chance after that," Mag said trying to stop him. "Alerting Ian can't help us.... Let's think of something else."

The woman's hand halted delicately on the man's hand and contained it; then they moved down together, leaving the alarm key untouched. The woman's eyes met the man's eyes. Slowly, Dan felt how she was sneaking at his breast in soft feline movements, how she was embracing him with her free arm. Her hot heavy breath burned his face for an instant, then her lips met his in an electrifying kiss. The touch felt like a nervous shock, and stiffened him.

Long afterwards, when the woman's eyelids began to lower heavily, covering her eyes, he was able to recover his senses. He freed himself hastily and backed a few steps staring at her in amazement.

"What was that?" he shouted.

Mag was looking at her fingers drumming on her multifunctional belt. A slight blush had appeared on her face and long delicate neck. She opened her mouth as if to speak, changed her mind, then opened it again, looking stealthily from under her long slightly upturned eyelashes.

"Don't look at me! Don't stare at me, please!" Dan shouted again, his eyelids tightly closed.

Mag tried to say something but the man was quicker.

"Tell me, how did you do it?"

"...."

"How did you manage to do that?" Dan said somewhat more calmly and turned to the wall, obviously trying to avoid the woman's gaze.

"Do what?" Mag burst out, letting herself fall into an armchair. Her blush had disappeared and only the balancing leg crossed over the other betrayed her agitation.

"A few moments ago," said Dan in a calm voice

now, "you hypnotised me, you can't deny that. Right after you fixed your eyes on me I could not move at all. Everything came back to normal when you closed your eyes."

It was the woman's turn now to look amazed. Then she looked thoughtful, preoccupied. One of her long thin eyebrows rose inquiringly, while her small lips pursed. If Dan had turned around to look at her, he would have sworn Mag was trying to whistle.

"OK, I'll try to explain. You can walk backwards if you want...."

"Towards you?"

"That's right. I want to show you something first."

"If you want to show me you know how to hug, I'd rather stay here and listen."

"Don't worry, I won't do it again. Your reaction spoke volumes. I've learned my lesson."

"I thought so. You can't inherit such techniques from your parents, you get them the hard way."

Mag's sound laughter made Dan accept the game. He began to move backwards in small steps, guided by the woman's voice. At last her arms halted on the man's hips, pulling them down towards her, at the same time inviting his hands to touch her waist.

"No!" Dan said. "Not again!"

Mag laughed again, more heartily.

"Don't panic," she whispered into his ear. "Try to guess what you touch."

The game went on, with the astronaut's hand going over Mag's belt. Each time he came across something, he said.

"Memoriser, opening button, energy piles, watch, individual access card, transmitter, call button, pulse and temperature display, biostim—Well, well, well. Since when have you been using biostimulators?" He turned towards her holding the small silvery tube in his hand.

"Since we started planning this thing. You can't realise the pressure Eva and I have been under," Mag pointed to her friend who was fast asleep at the other end of the room. "The biostimulator did it. I never knew how much it could increase my psychic and metabolic activity. First I wanted to prevent you from alerting Ian. Then I felt the need to embrace you. I felt the need so badly that my eyes, full of that psychic force, must have hypnotised you." She paused and added hesitatingly. "I suddenly felt something come over me wiping out all other thoughts and feelings. That something made me go for your eyes, for your body, and lose myself in them. As you can see, you've got your share of guilt too," she finished insinuatingly, watching the man's reaction.

After a while Dan spoke in a voice in which surprise had given way to a new, conciliatory tone.

"I've seen what a biostimulator can do to a woman who's never used it before. An interesting lesson for me. Interesting enough to ask you never to use it again." And then smiling. "With something like that, your psyche's a real social danger. Promise?"

Mag kept silent. Only her eyes lit up waggishly,

her face like that of a spoiled child grimacing at the thought of an unavoidable punishment. At last she nodded slowly, like a humanoid robot.

Dan threw the silvery tube away and said drily.

"OK...let's see what you can do without it."

* * * * * * *

Ted was awake but he did not know what was happening. He had a dim claustrophobic sensation. He felt that his body was different, more real, knitted together into a unified whole. The sensation of scattering, of inter-penetration with space was banished. That strange feeling had been as if his body was not quite his own, but in some indefinite borderline away from him. Ted lacked something, that sixth sense. Until now that had linked him to the exterior. Slowly he realised that he was alone, completely alone. There were no more hazy signs of the Varyan's presence coming to him. His isolation was complete.

A freezing fear sneaked into his heart, climbing up, throttling him. He groaned and fainted. Or seemed to faint for he soon discovered that he was still conscious after all. He was recovering, realising there was no more telepathic link, nothing left of that strange field. His interlocutor must be in trouble, he seemed to have told him something about that.

What could he do now? Establish a contact himself? Whom with? What should he focus on? He knew a few things about how to get into the state. A long time ago he had tried to send a message telepathically, and failed. He was a good receiver, though. He had to act now, else he would lose his mind. He had no other choice but to try. He focused. It was like listening hard, almost painfully, to that complete silence.

After a long while he seemed to hear a kind of rustle which did not resemble at all the previous telepathic perceptions; it sounded rather like a continuous whisper, similar to that made by a noise generator in the phonic laboratories. It was like nothing so much as a multitude of random but pleasant frequencies, undulating rhythmically, enveloping his temples.

Ted was happy. He felt the strange desire to abandon himself to that noise, he wanted his ears to open more, to capture more and more. It was like a dream. He had plunged into an immense ocean, whose waves were breaking against his temples, pushing him gently into an unreal world. There, he dared open his mouth under the surface. It was good. Now the whisper was all over him. He opened his eyes. Billions of glow-worms of all colours were dancing in front of him, getting into his eyes and then leaving again. He felt he was changing into a pulsating wave. He was the noise, the heat, the light, he was space itself. He was sinking into nothingness, following an irresistible call.

With a last glimmer of reason, Ted realised that he was now what he had always wanted to be: a particle of the cosmos, in the midst of a galactic nebula that was opening its arms made of the central star cloud with hallucinating speed. He was the middle of that star cloud, he was loosening himself into spinning arms, he was scattering himself among them in space, he was the Universe.

* * * * * * *

The huge heavy gnashing trap door moved replacing the light of day with an overwhelming shadow which swallowed the last of the sun's rays up. The elevator began to slide down faster and faster and a dim light told the scout team they could remove their protective glasses and mantles. They were underground again, away from the luminous flux that deranged their senses so violently.

Hor moved more slowly than the others. His long thin antennae were motionless, stuck to one another, in a unique order, a distinctive sign of his position as leader of the mission. He looked concerned about the report he had to write. The data they had been collecting would certainly give rise to passionate debates. Firstly, they had not been able to contact Sit. Then there were the alarming movements of the advanced troops in the North which could mean imminent conflict. Thirdly, there were the bizarre motionless groups of several hundreds of Trills, slightly semi-spherical in shape and divided by small sinuous canals.

Hor had never seen something like that before. He knew that at Level 6 of the underground city he lived in they were doing research on Trills. He also knew that the research had something to do with the messages that Sit kept sending from beyond the Varyan equatorial circle. They had been friends, he and Sit, before the scientist had been sent on that mission to the North. Hor was sure Sit had been sacrificed for the perpetuation of the mock-scientific co-operation between the two races designed to postpone the moment of confrontation as much as possible.

They were both fighting now for the same cause—to preserve the Varyan race. But Hor was not a scientist, he was a soldier, a professional. In that capacity he thought the Varyans did not have much chance to survive an open conflict with the Trills who were a hundred times more numerous than they were.

Except for Sit, Hor knew only the scientists that he had worked with on improving the defensive weapons. All the scientists and technicians were guilty of the great separation. They were living better here—so what? They were freer here—so what? Multiplication was a universal right, so was access to information, or to a leader's position at any level. Religious constraints were a thing of the past; they had given way to the free-thinkers who made up most of the refugees.

On the other hand, the northerners were passing through a period of stagnation. They were under strict repressive control which, sooner or later, would lead to confrontation with the South. Hor knew that was going to happen and he had to organise the Varyans so that they would believe in their chance of survival. He knew the fight would be ruthless, fought with terrible weapons.

The elevator's halt broke his meditation. The door opened and the team stepped onto a descending winding passage which led to a huge room full of bright signs pointing to corridors of different sizes, in many directions. Hor left the rest of the team and stepped on a moving belt. That took him to a similar but much brighter room, full of Varyans riding on quick vehicles. He relaxed, raised his antennae and breathed in the well-known light vibrations of the magnetic fields. He was in a familiar area. He entered a cabin and rushed forward to the information-sorting centre. He had to deliver the data to the internal circuit and then he could have a well-deserved rest.

* * * * * *

In his cabin, Olf was lying on a couch, staring at the ceiling, with his arms under his head. He had just finished thinking out the final details of the meeting which was to decide the rebellious level chief's inclusion in a forced anabiosis program until the expedition returned to the Earth. He was not going to be there to savour his victory, but he was content with what he had now. So far no one and nothing had stood in his way. He could not allow a younger member of the crew to influence the destiny of this complex. Dan had defied authority; he had made the mistake of making his position public against the man who held the power. Therefore, he had to bear the consequences. Olf did not know whether he was right or wrong—that was less important.

Then Olf heard the alarm. It took him only a few seconds to jump to his desk. He switched on all the means of data transmission but only the emergency ones responded. He rushed to the co-ordination centre and started giving curt orders to the supervision personnel. He checked the list of his senior subordinates on duty: very few were fitted for a situation like this. Dan was one of them and, as the ID card said, he was in his own cabin. He summoned them all and started collecting the data sent by the emergency circuits.

Olf's mind was invaded by dark thoughts. Someone was trying to restrict his access to information. The reports he was receiving from different areas were bewildering. As he ran through them, deep lines appeared on his forehead. He could not understand what was going on. The training courses he had attended had taken him through the most diverse situations, but what was happening now was impossible to relate to anything in his experience.

Slowly, hesitatingly, he went to the console, put in his ID card and pulled from the wall beyond a monolithic bloc with a small keyboarded panel in the middle. He started pressing "emergency," "security level," informational mechanism 1," "decision mechanism x," "intervention phase 3," "sabotage." Then he fed the information in the data file and pressed the expert program key. That very moment Dan made his appearance.

"Ten more seconds and you'd have been blocked somewhere along the way. Come, I think you've got something to say about what's going on."

"Yes, I can help you with some information," said

Dan thoughtfully, while two officers were setting the volition inhibitor around his forehead. The device was absolutely necessary in such exceptional circumstances.

Dan's sight got blurred, then dizziness made him stagger, while following the captain into the confidential cabin, completely isolated from the outside. There he heard Olf say.

"What no one could think of was the biotronic brain's quick reaction. Using a few robots it pulverised the armoured door of the Research Institute with some kind of thermic energy beam. Then a robot forced its way into the Council Chamber and broke the code of the recordings and decisions made by the ship chiefs during the last year. The next objective was the biology lab and I don't know why because, to me, the energy distribution system would have been more important. Then the biotronic brain took control of a group of robots at the intervention level, that know the complex quite well. They were quickly programmed to obey its radio orders and thus the brain's come to lead a small army."

"What have you done so far?" Dan asked, obviously impressed by what he heard.

"We've been jamming the brain's orders, but the frequencies keep changing. We've found out how the brain stopped the ordinary communication mechanism, and we hope to make it work again soon. We've completely isolated most of the levels with energy barriers which are hard to break, and we're trying to find what's happening in the navigation department."

"What, have they broken into the navigation depart-ment?"

"Look!"

Olf made the video-monitor light up and the room was invaded by the noises of a real battle on one of the access corridors between the levels.

"That's the main attack area of the security troops." The captain's voice turned as sharp as a knife. His body stiffened and only his eyes raced all over the screen.

Dan could hardly see anything. The power in the corridor had been cut. What seemed to be the attackers were using mobile spotlights to tear up the darkness, unveiling the thick curtains of smoke. The ventila-tion systems were probably out of use too as two huge ventilators were blowing fresh air along one of the walls and to the centre, making things somewhat visible. Thus Dan could make out some improvised obstacles—electro-cars turned upside down, massive faulty robots. From behind them men and robots were firing at one another.

The camp of the besieged seemed to be made up of robots only. Almost three quarters of them, of the humanoid type, were using light weapons with para-lysing rays. The others were providing the power and three or four, heavily armoured, were the mobile points of the barricade which they had raised in the middle of the access corridor. The paralysing rays convinced Dan of the intentions of the besieged. They were merely defensive. At a certain intensity the shocks did not kill but paralysed the victims' striated muscles, leaving their vital functions intact. The paralysed would be certain to spend several days in the recovery department.

The robots that were hit were pushed forward in order to enlarge the barricade. Their number was increasing steadily as the soldiers were merciless, launching missiles that exploded the moment they hit their targets, making fist-like holes into the robots. The loud cracks were accompanied by a thick smoke that was making the air almost opaque, coming in waves over the soldiers.

The searchlights brought out the sight of the rigid livid faces of the assault troops: security troops and soldiers in almost equal number. The wounded writhed a few seconds on the floor, shouting, before going rigid. The muscular spasms before paralysis looked terrible. The hallucinating dance of the searchlights suddenly revealed a soldier who had been hit right in the face. The dark burn in the corner of his mouth looked like a stigma of the stiffness of his entire body.

Dan stepped back instinctively, closing his eyelids tight at the horror. That rigid face, with its mouth wide open to release the cry of pain, with its eyes wide with fear, was nightmare itself. Everything was a nightmare. How was that possible? Who would have foreseen an almost pitiless battle between men and machines on one of the most daring missions meant to explore the Universe, millions of light-years from Terra?

He thought of the lab-ships they had used for the sociological tests. Many expeditions had perished to nothingness because of the disputes among the members of the crew. Those rival camps fighting for priority in decision-making appeared inevitably during long journeys.

They had taken account of all that. The biotronic brain was supposed to have run everything from beginning to end, by a clever game in which the crew's susceptibility had to be spared. The ordinator was supposed to have processed exact and if possible complete data so that the Council's decisions would be absolutely correct. Events, however, had brought a man to the leadership of the spatial complex. What could Olf really be thinking now? What did he think of the confrontation between the troops and robots guided by the ordinator? He, Dan, was tempted to believe that was a fight meant to keep a position and refuse the ordinator's return to the command of the ship.

The biotronic brain would not oppose the humans if it did not have good grounds to do it. The security of the crew and the aim of the expedition were its ultimate objective. The crew seemed to have forgotten that. Could it really be true? Could the ordinator have its own will? Could the neuronal cells have created for it a personality, and individuality similar to the human one? No, the original program had to be decisive, otherwise the whole expedition was going to perish.

Olf's theory could also be understood as an excuse for the captain's refusal to give up his position as leader of the ship. But Olf, for all his faults, was human not a machine. He seemed to be preferred for that. The entire crew was given the chance to refuse to submit to a monstrous ordinator, inhuman in its perfection and abilities. Yes, even if the ordinator had not malfunctioned, the same thing would have happened on another occasion.

How much the life of the whole crew had changed! A brilliant mind, an iron will, and a pride to match— that was the captain that had done it. A man who had now become most dangerous. Dan's knowledge of sociology made him see how the relations among the members of the crew were going to evolve if the initiative of the optotronic brain was neutralised. He did not have anything to reproach himself for. He had done the right thing in standing up to the captain. Unfortunately he could do nothing now. Everything seemed to depend on that bunch of machines on the screen. He could not help. He was himself in danger of being accused of taking part in unleashing these events.

He stepped towards the screen again, trying to make out the background. The besieged were less well-lit than the attackers. Not that they minded that. They guided themselves by infra red rays and tele-detection. Most of them moved more slowly than the humans and shot barrage salvoes. How long was their power supply going to last? The attackers were gaining ground anyway. New groups kept arriving, replacing the casualties. Ian was everywhere, shouting orders in his usual dry voice which sometimes covered the noises of the battle.

"I don't understand why Ian isn't using robots, too," Dan told Olf.

"He tried to, at the beginning," Olf's reply came after a while. "Too many losses. The rebels used disintegrators cleaning out the corridor with one salvo. We haven't got the time to make metal shields of heavy polinucleic atoms. We've got no other choice but to use the troops, which makes them use paralysing rays. As you know, the robots are programmed not to kill people."

Pretending he did not see the bitter smile at the corner of Dan's mouth, Olf continued in a changed voice.

"The assault isn't going to take long. We'll soon get to the command area. Look!"

Olf pointed to a dark spot on the screen towards which the troops were advancing. It looked like a door. Suddenly, a growing sinister rumble preceded a huge mass that hit the barricade forcefully and passed through it. It was a robot which had been brought from one of the workshops on the penultimate level.

Taking advantage of the surprise, the machine advanced through the door and stopped. Almost immediately the lower part of the robot opened and let a plasma burner out. From the opposite direction, a massive electro-car rushed at top speed against the robot. The impact produced a powerful explosion. The structure of the tunnel vibrated violently and made the picture on the screen shake. The two astronauts started and glanced at each other in panic.

Olf pressed a few keys and the picture appeared

again, this time from another angle. Both giants were motionless, one thrust onto the other, at a small distance from the burner which looked undamaged. In the next second Ian's order sounded powerfully in the acoustic translator.

"Fire!"

Hundreds of projectiles hit the robots at the same time, forcing the survivors to retreat and leave behind the smoking remains of those that had been fatally hit. Then Ian shouted a new order and a group of soldiers and technicians rushed to the burner and started to operate it. Presently, a reddish tongue licked the floor outlining grotesque shadows on the walls. Then the flame changed colour and focused on one spot arousing a shower of sparks and thick smoke. Dan could see the first drops of molten metal spreading out on the floor.

"One more hour and the optotronic brain'll lose the initiative. Then we'll make the final assault to the navigation room," Olf said.

"What kept you from getting there through the main passage?" Dan asked.

"The power installations—they've been extended to its walls."

"By whom?"

"By the robots from the power department."

"But what about the programs?"

Olf looked at Dan for a second, then back at the screen.

"The computer of the power department runs its own programs. Living matter can't fight them. But I've got a surprise for it. Our decoders are trying to break the command code. It's just a matter of time."

Dan saw the captain's hand gripping the edge of the monitor, its wrist whitening.

"Sabotaging machines! The guilty will pay, you can bet on that!" Olf shouted.

"Do you think one of us...?" Dan's voice trailed off.

Olf did not hurry to answer. Then he murmured as if to himself.

"The navigation room...."

"What's the matter with it? Do the personnel disobey your orders?" Dan's voice trembled against his wish.

"They claim they don't know what's going on in the command room."

"Claim?"

"The detectors are more than clear. They're all lying."

The news made Dan breathe deeply in an attempt to keep his balance. Olf felt his unrest and stared at him with icy eyes.

"It seems unlikely but there it is," he said.

"But it takes an experienced navigator to change the course of the ship."

"I wonder what the ordinator's up to. I wonder what the key to all its actions is," said Olf. "Let's go to the Council Hall and see what the others think about it."

On their way to the Council Hall, Dan tried to find his own answers to the captain's questions and his uncertainties.

"This biotronic brain seems to be more complex

than we wanted it to be. By implanting neuronal cells into it, its artificial intelligence acquired access to a new informational field."

Olf could hardly hide his astonishment.

"Go on," he said.

"An informational field which is characteristic of the living cells...from everywhere."

"Characteristic of any form of life? Even extraterrestrial?"

"Yes," Dan answered dryly without moving a muscle of his face.

"How do you know that?"

"I've just found it out today."

"Has that got anything to do with what's happening right now?"

Dan shuddered and said in a grave tone.

"Listen, there're quite a lot of scientists who think a bioenergetic field is attached to every being in the Universe—"

"Answer my question, damn it!"

Dan shook his head.

"Of course, it's the very cause of all our troubles."

"I don't understand."

Dan passed his tongue over his dry lips.

"Such a field can, under certain circumstances, interact with another one of the same type."

"It sounds logical. But how does it do it?"

"I don't know yet. Such an interaction's common to superior organisms which develop their awareness."

"The neuronal cells in the human brain?"

"That's right," said Dan, a shadow of a smile passing across his lips. "This galaxy, which I don't know if it was wise to cross, consists of huge concentrations of biofields. Our brains haven't been influenced by them, being the outcome of an evolution which has endowed them with informational networks able to capture inner and outer stimuli, memory, processing, transmission, and so on. Biofields play a rather insignificant part in these mechanisms. The biotronic ordinator's another kettle of fish, though."

Suddenly Olf found it hard to breathe. Dan went on.

"Not being part of an organism of the same structure, the living cells of the artificial intelligence have been powerfully exposed. They are virtually endowed with means of investigation characteristic of the ship itself."

Olf's eyes widened.

"Are you sure?"

"These galactic fields have acted upon the ordinator. Sensing their influence, the ordinator realised it could no longer run the ship and made us understand it had to be disconnected. Before disconnection, it recommended that we stuck to the course at steady speed until we reached the end of the galaxy. On leaving the galaxy we would have got rid of our troubles. But we didn't care about its recommendation. We stopped from time to time, did research, went on expeditions...."

The more than a hundred and fifty years of Olf's career were worth nothing in this situation, and the captain tried to hide that. His thin face looked resigned.

Dan said in a low voice.

"Then things happened as I presented them to the Council. On that routine mission Ted detected a strange form of life that uses biofields to exchange information on a large, almost exclusive, scale. It so happens that we've got a similar exemplar on the ship, in the space biology research complex."

"Ted disappeared on that planet in a catastrophe which was, to a large extent, brought on by himself."

"Yes, but...."

"Do you reproach me with the Council's decision?"

Dan did not understand what Olf was driving at.

"My reasons have always been justified," Olf said angrily.

"After such a long time, all of a sudden," Dan continued, "the creature goes through these changes, simultaneously with Tim's strange visions, in which Ted appears very clearly and very often, as if there were a telepathic bridge between him and the ship. Normally, Ted couldn't be alive—but what is normal here? I discussed this with Eva and Mag and we submitted our conclusions to the Council."

"What you did to the biotronic ordinator wasn't right at all...."

"So you know...," Dan stood still, coughed, and tried not to panic. "We just urged it to decipher the mystery of its own behaviour. First it wanted to take part in the research program. But when it realised it couldn't work with us, it took charge of everything."

"Do you think it'll give up?"

"No."

"Why?"

"Because finding the answer is vital for it."

"Do we have any chance to make it understand it's making a mistake?"

"I don't think so."

"Why?"

"It's probably convinced it's more competent than we are."

"Do you think it'd be a good idea to let it co-operate with us?"

"Why not? It seems to be our only chance to influence it."

Olf's voice sounded authoritarian.

"I will never allow a machine to impose itself on me! Both you and the two women have lost your sense of reality. Who knows what information you've supplied to the biotronic brain?! Or maybe you've tried to make it your ally?! Don't forget that I'm the captain of the ship! Very soon I'll have the situation under control. You know what's in store for you, don't you?"

Dan did not answer. He was just staring at nothing.

"Sabotaging and jeopardising the expedition's top priority objective will mean death for the three of you!"

Saying that, Olf stepped through the remains of the door to the large Council Hall.

* * * * * * *

"Hor!"

"...."

"Hor, wake up."

There was no answer from the low room in which the Varyan had taken refuge. Zeh showed his eagerness by fumbling through his sack and taking out with two of his suckers a small magnetic flashlight. The thin beam swept the walls until it finally focused on Hor's antennae which were fanned around him on the floor. The Varyan reacted violently. Beating the air with one of his soles and interposing it in the beam's way, he whistled slowly.

"What's going on? Who is it? Who let you in?"

"No one. Just your own interests," Zeh answered coldly. "You'd better get up. There're several commissions waiting for you. And they seem to have lost patience. A personal hearing's always very important. Also, there's a whole army of experts trying to find you on the surface. The research centres are in a terrible fever."

While Zeh was whistling hurriedly, overlapping his words, Hor got up slowly and felt the wall next to him. Presently, the click of a switch filled the room with a pale light which helped Hor make out his friend. Growling, he snatched the flashlight from Zeh's hands and let himself fall back to the mattress.

"Zeh, you've never been able to put facts into a logical order."

Zeh looked puzzled, his antennae moving around his mouth and finally stopping in a fan-like position. Hor went on evenly:

"Do you think I don't know what's happening? I've

come here because I don't know how many cycles'll have to pass until I can have another rest."

Hor's whistle got weaker.

"I admit there are a few things I can't understand, but they're insignificant. Tell me, what's the latest news about that extra-Varyan?"

"He was removed from his lab and no longer benefitted from the vitalising screen of the biofield. Sit did seem optimistic about it, though. He said it was likely that the monster no longer needed it. He's now able to create one by himself—a fraction of it's remained fixed on him reconstructing his original energy matrix. Sit was sorry he couldn't study him any more."

"What about the Trills?"

"They suspect we're experimenting on them in order to gain informational supremacy on the planet."

"What, do they already know about our research program?"

"Definitely not. It's just a hunch. Our program's so secret Sit himself doesn't know we've developed a part of his research work. The trouble is the northerners have begun to advance. We are at war. All the underground towns are on the alert. Mobilisation plans are being worked out. It seems they've reserved some very important missions for you. In fact, that's why I've come here. I wanted to learn something from you too. You tell me, I tell you. You know it's always been a fair trade."

Hor could not help smiling. Zeh had made a deal with him about exchanging information, which was the sign of great friendship on Var. A long time ago they had decided not to pay for it and just swap it. Now Hor had nothing to give Zeh, but he was extremely interested in what the latter knew. He grumbled indifferently.

"What I know is too important for me to accept an ordinary swap. You'll have to speak first. It could be something insignificant or worthless already."

There were a lot of loopholes in the Varyan laws concerning information. Legally, they had the right to know everything in their communities, but most of them held on to old mentalities which they had inherited from the northerners. Zeh was one of those who had made big hits at the information exchange, getting richer and richer. Now, although he was far from being gullible, he was going to give in, at least that was what Hor felt about him. And he was right. Curiosity was torturing Zeh. At last he decided to speak, though not in a direct way. He began.

"The groups of Trills you saw on the surface are transmission relays."

"What?" Hor started and got up from the floor.

Zeh noticed his reaction contentedly. He went on savouring the moment.

"Our decoders are working hard on their messages but they haven't come up with anything yet. However, I've managed to lay my hands on something. The thousand credits I've paid were worth it. Believe it or not, the big news is that one of the Trills is travelling through space. The groups of Trills on the surface are focusing their fields on the sky. It's obvious he's the target -"

Zeh was interrupted by Hor's reaction. His friend seemed to have gone mad—he was looking around the room for something to climb on. There was nothing but the floor in the room, though, and Hor, in his despair, hung on to Zeh with his soles, trying to climb on to him. One of his limbs blocked Zeh's mouth so Zeh could no longer speak. Hor had to free Zeh's mouth in the end but, while doing it, he lost his balance and fell to the floor. Among guffaws, Zeh whistled.

"You'd rather fall than hear me out."

"Oh, shut up! I mean go on," Hor said angrily.

"And now a piece of my mind. I think the Trill's on the flying machine which has sent the extra-Varyan here. It's the Trills that have given life to the extra-Varyan and read his mind. It's they who are making the connection between the monster and its siblings."

Zeh had to stop in order to put his suckers on Hor who was climbing the walls. With a sigh of gratitude Hor purred to the one below him.

"Thank you, Zeh. You're a real friend."

* * * * * * *

The molten edges of the sheet of metal and the burning smell made Dan shudder and stop in front of the ragged oval of the door. Olf had already passed through and stopped, blocking the view. Dan closed his eyelids tight. The excitement of the past three days had finally overcome him. It was now changing him into an amorphous mass of bones, flesh, and nerves, ready to accept anything, only to put an end to it all. He cared about nothing. His thoughts went back to the cabin on B Level in which he had left Mag. How cruel fate could be, after giving him those moments of happiness. Two hours, only two hours had been enough to make him feel different. "Strange," he murmured, "just when...."

Dan started. His thoughts were driven away by the noise coming from the large hall. At last he made up his mind and slightly pushed Olf aside so that he could pass. The captain moved docilely, like a robot. Puzzled, Dan looked at his face and saw it black with rage, his mouth contracted into a grotesque grimace. He was staring ahead at the wall facing him. There, huge on the screen, Lem was grinning. He was dressed in his pilot suit with the insignia of the navigation department commander.

"Come in, Dan. I think you're the only adviser here capable of explaining to the audience what I'm about to do," said the man on the screen.

With a triumphant smile, Lem zoomed the picture to small dimensions. The audience could see a desk dominated by a transparent box revealing a single key.

"I'm going to give the captain the chance to attend the launching of a program that's never before been launched on any of his previous ships. Come on, captain, try to look more solemn. It's a unique event, after all," Lem laughed sarcastically staring at Olf. "What astronaut belonging to the old generation has ever lived through such a moment? No one that

I know, though I do know three or four who would give anything, even the rest of their lives, for something like this. And here I am, the man you gave up so easily a few days ago, offering you this chance. It's a great pleasure and it comes from the fact that I am here again, where I belong. You belong here too, as a spectator, of course. Ha—ha—ha!" Lem's demonic laugh froze the blood in the veins of the entire audience. "Dan," Lem went on sharply, "take the old starwolf to his armchair and belt him to it. I don't want him to get into any trouble. Posterity might ask us to display him in some museum and I want to hand over the exhibit in a fairly good state."

Then Lem addressed the audience.

"As I explained to you earlier, the biotronic brain of the ship has appointed me provisional captain until his cells can be integrated into the decision-making mechanism. Right now, the brain's preparing the final data for the hyperspace leap. We all know that such a leap is very demanding in energy capital, but at the place we need to go there are extremely serious things happening that directly affect our interests. That's why, at least for the time being, the top priority objective of our expedition has been changed. In my new capacity, I assure you that it's essential to give the command of the complex to the biotronic brain. We will go back to the edge of this galaxy to clear up the mystery of its disorderly conduct. The new top priority objective will be the third planet of the KH-09 solar system where we lost Ted. You all remember the details of that terrible drama, I hope? Well, we have managed to contact rational beings that live on that planet. Or, to be more accurate, the biotronic brain has done it. It sounds incredible, but Tim, Ted's four-year-old son, has been contacted telepathically and our interpretation of the contact makes us believe that Ted is alive. Those rational beings have brought him back to life and seem to have established some kind of contact with him. Ted is in the very midst of a planetary conflict between life forms similar to the one we have in our space biology lab. Those life forms might help us puzzle out the anomalies of our biotronic ordinator. The fields in which they seem to be more advanced are biology and electromagnetic waves. It's very likely they use weapons based on radiations of light-stimulated beams. They will be hard to counteract in the atmosphere and on the surface of the planet where we cannot operate our gravitational shields easily."

Lem stopped for a second, then continued more quietly.

"But for the recent events on the ship, as well as the latest analyses of the biotronic brain, I wouldn't believe in what I am saying myself. I learned about all this a few hours ago, when the ordinator asked for my collaboration. I've seen Tim personally, as well as the creature in the lab, otherwise I wouldn't be here addressing you."

Recovering from the shock, Olf seemed to be considering the situation. He quickly reacted to Lem's last words.

"But why you?"

Lem looked as if he had not understood the question. Then his face eased into a broad smile.

"Because you chose me. The moment you dismissed me I started counting on the ordinator as a potential ally, together with Dan, Eva, and Mag. As you can see, there are four of us. Anyway, as navigator I am one of the few people on this ship able to operate a hyperspace leap."

"But...how are we to supplement the energy reserves?"

"The brain's already started the proper program."

"But...what you're doing now...."

"It's a first, but I'm in full control of everything. Look, the preparations have just finished. I'm sorry, I have to go now."

Lem disappeared from the screen. They had all managed to see the growing excitement in the navigation department, a sign that the preparations were finally over. Indeed, they felt a slight vibration in the ship's structure. At the same time, the sound and optical gauges let all the members of the crew know about the approaching change of the flight conditions.

The warning signals echoed in the silent hall. The audience was too surprised by the turn of events to be able to react in any way. Their roles had been reduced to that of helpless witnesses.

All of a sudden the giant level rings stopped spinning around the central fusiform body, and long thin threads sprang from behind the complex weaving into a strange texture. Almost immediately, they formed a huge funnel whose mouth framed the complex as if the latter wanted to swallow itself. After a slight tremor of the enormous structure, a big globe of plasma appeared shining violently for a moment, then vanished together with the ship.

Time and space in their impassivity witnessed a phenomenon as extraordinary and mysterious as their own existence. A material body detached itself from its co-ordinates and was instantly replaced by a gap more uncontained and deeper than the cosmic dream itself.

* * * * * * *

Hor was looking through the optic device at the flat uniform soil which stretched out several dozens of units above him. The landscape, blemished with the carbonised stains of the luminous impulses, seemed to belong to another world. A thick reddish smoke was looming over the horizon, the result of the southerners' riposte to the northerners' attack.

Thanks to the superior destructive force of his guns, Hor had held the position against the strength and number of the attackers. The latter had in truth seemed to be taken aback by the extraordinary fire concentration of the northerners. Hor himself wondered if he had not been more useful underground where the real battle was going on.

"Look! We're a real force, aren't we?"

The one who had just interrupted his train of thoughts

was Zeh. He was standing next to him, looking through a similar device. They could now glimpse long rows of thousands of Varyans marching towards the horizon line. Indeed, there was something grandiose about the scene. After the salvoes of luminous rays, Hor had gained room for manoeuvre in front of him which he hurried to occupy with vanguard troops.

"Who's ever accepted to give his life to defend some area full of huge groups of Trills?" asked Zeh rhetorically.

"You might be right," Hor murmured. "I wonder how important they can be to us. Those Trills are the remains of the northern colonies that have been destroyed by the Big Group troops. They just take shelter behind that line—and their number grows by the minute. The secret seems to lie in the installations the technicians mounted next to them."

"Tell me something, Hor. What do you expect to achieve here? The area around us is just flat land, without any strategic value. Does that justify the presence of a soldier of your stature and one of the biggest guns we've got?"

Hor did not answer right away and Zeh noticed a slight nervousness in him. His eyes stared at Hor following his agitated to-and-fro walk through the small shelter. Then Hor burst out.

"You know what? I'm full of doubts about my real role here." His antennae started moving in a disorderly manner. "Our troops here are exceptionally well-trained. I've never before commanded such elite units, with such redoubtable weapons at their beck and call. The light-gun's meant to keep the northerners at a distance for some time. The position, however, is not part of a general defence plan.... For two cycles now I've been worrying about the lack of strategic logic in our leaders' plans, about this useless sacrifice. That's why I've called you here. I wanted to know what you thought of it."

"Just for that? You must be joking!" Zeh's voice was trembling. "You promised me complete mystery, sensation, extraordinary events. Do you know how many strings I had to pull to get here? Do you know I haven't got the slightest idea about how I'm going to get back? Is that what you call a favour?"

Stimulated by the aggressiveness of his words, Zeh jumped from his place and swirled his limbs at Hor angrily.

"What the hell do you take me for?"

"One of the Varyans interested in plunging into the middle of some exceptional events."

Hor had calmed down as if he had transferred all his unrest to the other. He stared hard at his friend with a hypnotic look in his eyes. After a few moments of silent confrontation, Zeh's look became tired and yielding.

"I don't want to stay here any longer. You guaranteed my safety as long as you controlled the position. I think you won't be able to send me back later so I'd better leave—"

A powerful explosion interrupted him, shaking the walls of the shelter. It was followed at once by the wailing chorus of the alarm sirens, which was accompanied by a sequence of more and more violent noises—long heavy whizzes of an incredible intensity. While Zeh cowered in a corner, his limbs and suckers covering his rolled-up antennae, Hor climbed onto the observation platform and looked through the optic device.

He took his time, his feelings showing on his skin kneaded by convulsions. At last, when the noises stopped, the Varyan climbed down slowly, his eyes closed, prey to the strangest of visions. He made for the box of instructions and opened it as if in a trance.

"What're you doing?" Zeh's thin voice broke the unnatural silence of the shelter.

"This is a set of provisions I wasn't supposed to read until the next cycle."

Hor's suckers revealed several tubes which contained documents carrying the seal of the supreme scientific and military forum. Zeh dared to climb onto the observation platform and hesitatingly put his eyes to the optic device. He did not have the time to see anything because Hor shouted at him.

"Don't look! It could be too much for you. It wasn't a northerners' attack. The sunlight's turned blue. Or rather, a blue sun's gone down behind the line. Everything's changed. The ground's full of holes. If that's what I think it is.... Here, have a look at this."

A document changed hands quickly. Zeh read it while Hor went on.

"The forecasting signs, our exact co-ordinates,

everything connects now. Only it's happened sooner than expected."

"You knew it, didn't you?" Zeh glanced at Hor with foggy eyes.

"No, it was just a hunch, one of those hunches you don't dare admit even to yourself."

"And now? What shall we do now? The contact-organising commission is still far away."

"I've got an idea," said Hor and made for a trap-door. "Come along. The war's over for us. No one can prevent us from accomplishing another mission. I promised you extraordinary events, didn't I? We've got the unique opportunity to be the first Varyan messengers to contact another world. It's them, Zeh. They're here...."

* * * * * * *

"What about the grav fluxes, Andy?"

"Grav field of lowest oscillation! All machines under control!"

"All right, Andy," Gil muttered, slightly irritated by the android's monotone voice. The suppliers had forgotten how boring a universal voice synthesiser could be. He looked out of the corner of his eye at the machine sitting in the chair beside him. The android was sitting upright, his eyes fixed on what they had to be. These "Andys," they were all good boys...and reliable.

The memo started buzzing discreetly. Gil pressed the key for the navigation room of the intergalactic complex.

"Hi, Lem. How's the signal?"

"Hi, Gil. Not bad at all. Look out for the fields!"

"Don't worry. I'm luckier than Ted. Besides, I'm not alone, am I, Andy?"

The android nodded and said as if dying to be noticed.

"Ground takes a rather unstable landing. Area free of obstacles."

"Look around, Andy. I don't want to get out of this on all fours."

"Change of co-ordinates forbidden. Area chosen by the hosts," said Andy imperturbably.

"Hey, who's the boss here?"

"Stick to the program, Gil," said Lem. "And please be on the lookout. The beings meeting us are waging a war. And don't forget the protective barriers."

"You can afford to give advice from up there, can't you?" Gil's voice sounded a little uncertain. Emotion and strain were growing while the surface of the planet became clearer through the portholes of the module. "If only I knew what they look like...."

"Sorry, Gil," Lem said. "You'll have to manage by yourself."

"Yeah, I know. We, pioneers, who loiter for years and years on the complex to be asked overnight to deal with the most inconvenient situations. Come on, Andy, let's go down!"

The module shook a little as if greeting the clouds and started to fall. Almost without any hesitation, it landed on a field that seemed to have been marked artificially.

Gil heard the android's voice again.

"Correct landing."

"Great," Gil said with a sigh of relief that could not hide his tension. "Did you hear that, Lem?"

No answer. The spotlights were sweeping the ground around to compensate for the weak light which seemed to come from the low layer of clouds. Gil looked through the portholes and cursed his predicament. He had to contact an extraterrestrial civilisation and did not know how. Worse than that, he had been warned of the possibility of an attack. He had no other choice but to find whatever solution he thought fit. Anything was possible. Ted had got into trouble on exactly the same kind of module and the same kind of planet. Had the natives shot him down? An accident was almost ruled out, Ted had been one of the best...but he had been all by himself.

"Hey, Andy! How about going out for a walk? I'll stay here and cover."

The android did not hurry to reply. He was probably trying to find in his program a behaviour pattern or a prior experience to use under these circumstances. Gil found himself smiling. Andy could not find that, he was sure. The android would have to be manoeuvred like a puppet.

"Come on, just go round the ship and come back. That's all you've got to do."

While the android was getting ready to leave, Gil

took another look outside and noticed a weird figure moving slowly towards the module.

"Lem! Lem! There's something coming towards me, Lem!"

"What does it look like? Does it look aggressive?"

"I can't say. I can't say anything yet. The creature looks shapeless, it's about half our size—I think it's covered with something—anyway, it's brightly coloured.... I don't feel like having it too close."

"Ready to go out," the android said and the creature stopped as if it had heard his words.

It was now a hundred, a hundred and fifty metres away from them. It seemed to be spinning around without coming any nearer, undecided. Gil thought of the rituals of primitive human communities but then he realised that was a creature that had been waiting for him and communicated somehow with the ship's ordinator. It could be anything but primitive.... Suddenly his head emptied of all the instructions he had learned for such moments. Somewhere, behind that creature, he saw another one. He had to make up his mind.

"Andy, go out, approach the first creature, but do not step beyond the protection field. Wave your arms about like some kind of greeting. I want to see its limbs, its head, and whatever it's got apart from that shapeless body. If they're clever, they'll have to respond somehow. And remember: no heroics. You're just reconnoitring. Understand? Just reconnoitring."

* * * * * * *

The aliens' ship was the first thing Hor saw on leaving the tunnel. Zeh had stayed behind, maybe he did no want to come at all, but Hor did not care. He was staring at the metal colossus ahead. There was something inexplicable drawing him towards that thing. After a moment of hesitation, he made the first move. Then another and another. Nothing happened. Finally, he found himself advancing as fast as he could, in spite of the heavy equipment he was carrying.

A stifled noise coming from behind made him stand still. He turned round. It was Zeh, trying hard to catch up with him.

"Are you afraid to stay down there by yourself?" Hor asked.

Zeh did not answer; he just waved excitedly to something that had got out of the ship. It was an alien, huge, about three times taller than they were, with very few limbs which were amazingly long. Hor burst out laughing nervously.

"Hey, what's that? It uses two limbs for walking... and no suckers...."

Hor felt the need to get closer. Then he sensed the field. It was vast and curved, seeming to surround the ship. Energy of the best quality. Hor's antennae stretched out and absorbed the food.

"A real feast, isn't it?" he said.

Zeh joined him saying, "It's incredible. They've guessed our tastes. What we've got here's enough for dozens of cycles...."

"Yeah, but it's bad manners to have too much of it....

Look! It's going back!"

Hor made one step ahead and felt it. The alien was made up of a tangle of weak pulsating fields altogether different from what he had imagined. He whistled forcefully.

"I wish you welcome, being from another world! My name is Hor."

Instead of replying, the alien sent a flux of waves towards the ship. Hor whistled again. The alien sent a flux towards him which explored his body carefully, methodically. The Varyan understood the other one was examining him and decided to wait patiently, although the radiation made him itch. Then the surprise came. The alien gave out a long whistle, powerfully modulated and perfectly correct.

"I wish you welcome, being from another world! My name is Hor."

The Varyan lost his balance—it was his own voice.

"Hor!" Zeh had overcharged himself and stretched his antennae out to the alien. "That's not a being. It's a machine, an automaton."

Hor raised his eyebrows, bewildered.

"Yet, it greatly resembles the description we got from Sit."

"It doesn't matter. Don't you feel it? It's an artificial structure...."

The alien did not try to advance but waved to them with two of its limbs.

"Hor...we've got to know if that machine's alone, if that's its only ship...."

"I don't think so.... What would you do if you were them? Would you expose yourself from the very beginning, just like that? It seems to be a messenger, rather...."

"I think we should make it understand we want the real ones, not the machines."

"Agreed. But how?"

The Varyans made for the ship pretending to ignore the android that, in the meantime, had called Hor again. Once in front of the ship, they had to wait for quite a while until another alien appeared at last. It was shorter and started to move clumsily towards them.

Zeh became nervous.

"Look! Can you feel it?"

Hor nodded, staring at the newcomer. Signals of weak but definite biological activity were reaching them in an irresistible call that made them forget all fear or restraint. It was the call of rational fellow-creatures.

PART II

Truth is a dark and deceitful thing.
Anthony Boucher

Hor was waiting in the reception room. The new southern Council had finally made up its mind to answer the statement he had made some time ago. Hor did not accept the new political leadership. He had spoken his mind about that, submitting to a self-banishment until he received the official reaction.

After long debates, the new southern Council had chosen to summon him. Hor had got ready for the meeting in the traditional style: sitting on the floor, his immobile arms covering his soles. This position helped him concentrate and, at the same time, would force his interlocutor to get straight to the point.

All of a sudden, he sensed someone approaching. He became alert. Sooner than he expected, he saw the door move and reveal a funny stout Varyan. Instead of his antennae there was a big dark swelling, surrounded by holes from which sprang sinuously towards the tip numerous fine scales.

Hor greeted the Varyan ceremoniously waving his antennae and savoured the obvious confusion of the newcomer, unable to reply with the same gesture. Embarrassed, the latter just moved his eyelids across his eyes several times. Then Hor said mockingly.

"Your position in the new Council looks more than conspicuous. Pity the implant couldn't completely replace the antennae you gave up so easily."

"Soon we'll all have implants. They will stop marking out the personalities of the leadership. They will defeat the conservatism and stupid inertia of—"

The newcomer stopped, fearing his words might offend the soldier. Hor did not even blink. He had already drawn his conclusions: he was not dealing with an elite Varyan; the uncontrolled movements of the other's skin disgusted him. He remembered how many times he had lost his temper against his own will, experiencing so many awkward moments. Now he enjoyed thinking that was a thing of the past and found himself smiling. The other took it as a sign of good will and went on.

"I am the bearer of the answer to your statement."

The soldier's reaction was unexpected.

"What's my statement got to do with you? Who gave you access to its contents?"

"I think you misunderstood me," the Varyan said quite surprised. His limbs cut the air stretching above his head anxious to brush his antennae which were no longer there. His suckers felt the ragged surface of the implant for a second, then fell to his soles, together with a nervous whistle.

"I think...you're taking me for someone else. I'm an

official, I've been empowered to have a very important discussion...."

Hor's eyes were full of contempt. The soldier kept quiet for a while, then replied sententiously, as if making a last concession to the Varyan in front of him.

"I think my statement's too important to discuss with you here. That's all I've got to say."

"As you wish. You should know, however, that the new Council doesn't agree with your views; in spite of that, it's willing to overlook them. More than that, it's willing to co-operate with you." The Varyan held out a long box and put it down, next to one of Hor's soles. "You must admit that the old Council could not cope with the latest developments. The new Council is of the same opinion as you are—there's no authority now able to control the changes that are taking place.... You should appreciate that, shouldn't you?"

Hor kept sitting on the floor as immobile as before, his eyelids tightly covering his eyes. Only the corner of his mouth was slightly trembling with contempt.

"I see that you categorically reject the presence of the new order. You probably think it's influenced by the northerners. Well, let me tell you that most of the society is on our side. We will keep our promises. We will give a new meaning to our existence and our relations with the cosmic beings. We will reconsider our position as far as the war against the northerners is concerned. Discipline and submission to authority will be a fact. The true elite will decide the others' fate— but not by swimming in the huge question mark and the technocrats' useless quest. We will conduct the evolution on Var in the right direction, without tolerating any deviations. You can already see how easily they all give up the false freedom they thought they enjoyed in order to acquire the certainty of an inflexible authority. This authority will spare them the trouble of making choices all the time."

Upset by Hor's lack of reaction, the Varyan paused to recover his breath. He hesitated between the wish to continue and the more realistic alternative of leaving the room. He chose the latter. Turning to the door, he said.

"If you refuse collaboration, you'll have to accept the exile you're deliberately trying to adopt. This time, however, the exile will be inevitable. You will be nothing but an ex-soldier.... But again, you can join us and your influence will be immeasurable, one of the most powerful on the entire planet. You decide!"

After the Varyan left the room, Hor remained in the same position. Only the black box in front of him proved that someone else had been there. He stared at it, then he raised it slowly to eye-level and opened it. There were a lot of carefully folded papers there, a spiralled strip above them. Two suckers unrolled the strip. Hor skimmed over the message without showing any reaction. Only when he finished reading it and saw the signature did he start a little. It was Zeh's. His old friend, an important political leader now, was asking him to co-operate in a crucial program.

Why him? Hor knew he was one of the best soldiers;

however, he had proved hard to co-operate with. The questions' vicious circle jumbled his thoughts at a reckless gallop. How extraordinary the consequences of those beings' arrival on their planet were! Hor and Zeh, the first Varyans to meet them, had not been able to anticipate them either. And all these papers in the box.... He quickly took them out and spread them all around him, skimming over their contents. His antennae started to draw restless circles in the air as a sign of his concentration.... Eventually, all his uncertainties vanished giving way to exaltation. After a special briefing, Hor was to enter the northern camp as representative of the southern Council and start negotiations. This mission could mean the end of the war.

* * * * * * *

Lem was at the end of a steady effort which had been interrupted only by meal breaks and energising treatment. He had in turn replaced three teams of navigators and informaticians in his attempt to decipher the labyrinth of the central memory store. Only the general structure had been preserved—the biotronic brain had re-organised and replaced numerous subunits throughout its existence. Allowing the astronauts to access its contents directly, the machine reminded Lem of a man letting the others read even his most intimate thoughts. Lem had finally succeeded in reconstructing the intergalactic ship's entire route to the Varyan orbit—more than eighteen years of travel.

He found Dan among the members of B square.

"Finished at last," he said with a sigh of relief.

"Congratulations. Now we can finally launch the probe."

"Bloody machine! We've all been the victims of its whims, if you can imagine that!"

"Not a simple machine at all, eh?"

"You can say that again. The hyperspace leap seems to have aroused the most conflicting reactions in the ordinator. I could swear it's hiding a few things from us. And it didn't shrink from making it clear it knows much more than we do.... And this new Varyan Council, I wonder how they came up with this idea of the message?"

"I don't really know. It seems a legitimate wish, though. They send a message to the civilisation that's contacted them through its messengers."

"That is us."

"Exactly. Though the term doesn't completely cover our position."

"Who could really define it after so many compromises? If the initiators of our expedition knew what we're doing here, on Var...."

Lem did not seem to wait for an answer. He just switched the link off making Dan think he would resume the conversation when they were face to face. Which was partly true. Lem had always distrusted the Varyans' good intentions as expressed in their official statements.

* * * * * *

The caterpillars were stirring up a column of dust which was settling back quietly in undulating waves. The strong light, the suffocating temperature, the bumpy ground, and the lack of vegetation upset the Varyan, to say nothing of the small cabin of the vehicle which limited his movements. Nothing had happened so far and that was his only comfort. It had been a long journey and it did not seem it would end soon. He was already passing through the negotiated area but no northerner had made his appearance yet. He cursed the blocked underground tunnels. These would have spared him the fatigue of a slow uncomfortable surface trip.

Hor had never been here before. The enemy territory in this part of the planet was as unknown to him because of the result of the mission he had been sent on by the new southern Council. Zeh had been by far the most persistent member of the council. He as well as all the other councillors had placed enormous responsibilities upon his shoulders. They knew that his meeting with the northerners would be decisive and that made Hor nervous. It was funny that his honest stand and constant refusal to yield to the temptation of a political career had made him the most commendable southerner for such a mission. At least, that was what they had thought. As for him, Hor knew he was just a good soldier. And a good strategist. But what he was supposed to do now went far beyond the competence of an ordinary soldier.

The fact that he had accepted the mission was due to

the great stakes in play. And his unexpected appoint-
ment coming from all the factions of the council.
Stability, unity of views, no longer existed in the south.
They had been shattered by that extraordinary event—
the appearance of the Earthling astronauts. Had that
had the same effect on the northerners, he wondered?
The negotiations would no doubt depend a great deal
on that.

Thus sunk in thought, Hor reached an area where a
strong wind was sweeping the dry ground, obstructing
the view with thick whirlwinds of dust. He stopped the
vehicle, took his guiding instruments and went out. He
was too busy trying to find out where he was to see the
northern patrol surrounding him quietly. He heard the
warning shout and looked up.

They were big, wearing a strange uniform, perfectly
adapted to surface life. It was a sort of silvery sack
which made their dark eyeglasses and antennae-
protecting helmets stand out. They did not seem to be
carrying weapons. Not the kind of weapons he had
expected them to be carrying anyway.

They examined him in silence. Then they started
shooting questions which were always ahead of the
intruder's short answers. Things might not have ended
too well for Hor if he had not mentioned Orm. The
name seemed to be awe-inspiring for immediately the
patrol formed a broad circle around him—here the
importance given to a Varyan was measured by the
distance which the others put between him and themselves. Hor had been warned of this oddity and smiled

slightly remembering the detail.

Respectful, suspicious silence set in the ranks of the northerners' patrol. Presently, the leader contacted the base. His sudden reaction, as well as that of the others, baffled Hor: they started running backwards in a disorderly way, trying hard to put as much distance as possible between themselves and the newcomer. Hor saw in consternation how the circle was broadening, how the hurried, funny movements of the northerners' soles were leaving long trails on the ground, and heard the indefinite panicky whistle coming from the slower ones.

Then he understood and began to laugh. It was a noisy and at the same time controlled laughter which made his whole body shake, resembling a nervous discharge. Now he could afford to look in complete detachment at that bunch of natives. The distance was too big for dialogue but neither he nor the others seemed to regret that. It was the maximum distance at which an acceptable visual contact could be kept.

Hor looked around. Somewhere, not far from his vehicle, he saw a long object with metallic reflexes propped against one of the many rocks that dotted the ground. It had obviously been left there by one of the members of the patrol. He went up to it and raised it: it looked like a guiding tube, equipped with a sophisticated optic system and a control mechanism which seemed easy to operate. At the other end, the weapon—for it was undoubtedly a weapon—had a tank and an intermediate chamber, probably for regulation or dosage. He pointed it clumsily at a rock in front of him. Then he fired. Nothing happened. The release made a slight buzz and that was all. He examined the weapon again. It was light, very light, made of an unknown material. The effect was not visible at all. How did it work?

As if to enhance his confusion, a huge vehicle appeared on the horizon and covered the distance in no time, making the rocks and the air roll. Then another and another, passing by him at a giddy speed to finally stop in a triangle that framed him almost perfectly. Hor looked at them in bewilderment. A powerfully amplified whistle came out of the three vehicles.

"Our master Hor is kindly asked to put the weapon down. He does not know how to handle it yet."

Hor felt he needed all the self-control he could muster. He focused and at last managed to recover. He put the strange weapon down beside him. The next moment a module came off one of the vehicles and moved smoothly up to him. From within a small northerner emerged, supple and agile. He was wearing a flexible sack-like helmet. His long, very long, antennae waved at the newcomer several times, then settled in ascending levels, supported by upturned limbs. All except one which grabbed the weapon. The northerner glanced at it, then at Hor, then at the weapon again, with an embarrassed, guilty smile on his face. He noticed the dark patch on the rock and understood. He pushed the rock slightly with one of his soles. At once the rock was replaced by a pile of fine dust, scattered by the breeze blowing from behind.

"Our master Hor is kindly asked to hurry. He is anxiously expected," the northerner said and waved to the module from which he had emerged.

* * * * * * *

Lem had been for quite a while in the company of the B square members. They were all standing around a high pedestal.

"I've provided the space required by the Varyans here, in the middle third." The spotlight operated by Dan moved quickly over the model of the space probe which was to be the go-between of the two civilisations. "In the first third we are going to put the auto-pilot, the robot, and the trajectory-guiding program. In the last third we'll have to place the anti-grav generator and the regenerative batteries."

"Do we have such a big robot?" asked a member of the crew.

"Of course. It's the robot of the probe itself. The alterations we've made are not major. It's been much harder to increase the abilities of the auto-pilot, though," said Lem looking at the model. "Pity we'll have to launch the probe from where we made the hyperspace leap. The distance between that spot and Var is about five million parsecs."

"What's its mass?"

"About ten thousand tons when at rest."

"That much? What will the Varyans fill the space with?"

"We don't know for sure. They did ask for the equivalent of two hundred cubic metres, which will take more than six million tons of material."

"A few dozen frozen Varyans plus all their installations would get there easily. And that would still take only a fifth of the space they asked for," said Dan and shrugged.

"You don't understand a thing, do you?" said Lem and laughed. "I don't understand it either. We've just met their requests, that's all."

"Yes, but...what about the five million parsecs? How do you think that distance'll be covered?"

"By a hyperspace leap."

"Is it really that simple?"

"It sounds incredible, but it's simpler than you think. You know the biotronic ordinator made some sensational discoveries during the hyperspace leap. All of them are related to the ordinator's identification with the ship itself. Just as you, for instance, learned the weightless mechanical flight, with all the reflexes and techniques it involved, the ordinator 'caught' the secret of the hyperspace leap."

"That's too hard to believe," said Dan fretting. "Have you thought of a plausible explanation?"

"Of course. The anti-grav engines allowed it to slide along the lines of the gravitational field while being in permanent contact with them."

"That's not enough. Try again."

"OK. Just listen. By consuming energy, the engines can alter, to some extent, these gravitational lines in order to control and stabilise the trajectory of the ship. How do you go down vertically without changing your orientation horizontally?"

"Hmm...I create a conic vortex and place myself at its base, then I cut off the air transversally, with the wings at right angles."

"Perfect," Lem nodded, a satisfied smile on his face. "So you alter the movement of the air surrounding you to get the trajectory you want. Now imagine that, just as they put mechanical wings on you so you could learn the basic movements, I showed the ordinator the basic manoeuvres for the hyperspace leap. Using its extraordinary intuition and ability to analyse everything in infinitesimal time, it soon 'caught' the technique."

"And what's that technique?"

"The ship just 'comes off' the gravitational lines against which it leans while moving. That's similar to the fall of a bird around which you suddenly create an advanced vacuum. At this stage, time and space get different from what we know them to be."

"I know. Time stops dead and—"

"In the next stage, the ship 'sticks' to another gravitational line and, by doing that, it gets a new time-space co-ordinate which can be more or less different from the original ones. Thus the ship jumps to another place from where it can continue its journey either by using the surrounding gravitational lines or by flying at sub-light speeds."

"And how is all that energy consumed?" asked Dan.

"Most of it is consumed when the ship comes off the

initial time-space co-ordinate and joins the new one. The ship virtually detaches from and attaches itself to the surrounding universe. That stops Time as we know it. During the leap, Time can't be measured because it disappears pure and simple. It's for this stoppage of time that we pay the price of such a heavy energy consumption."

"But we do save time by that, don't we?"

"Well, it's more like we gain time."

"What do you mean we gain time?"

"We gain time by changing the direction of Time's arrow. It's the only case when we have that."

"And how much time did we reverse making this leap of five million parsecs?" asked Dan, a little upset by the navigator's patronising tone.

"About a week. We got here about a week before the leap. That corresponds to about a Varyan cycle. Do you remember the southerners were taken aback by our arrival? That soldier who met us when the ship landed admitted later that in no way could he understand one thing: how we got there about one Varyan cycle before the leap that was to take us there. He didn't know Time would reverse, forced by the energy consumed and the distance annulled instantaneously.... The fact that the Varyans knew about our arrival is quite extraordinary. Someone must have told them the exact date of the leap, but he didn't take into account the change in Time's axis. Whoever that was we'll probably never know," said the navigator in a slightly rhetorical tone.

"Hmm...," said Dan and glanced at Lem ironically.

"You've heard about those weird creatures in the space biology lab, haven't you?"

"You mean the Trill?"

"No, I mean the Trills! Now there are more of them. Some say the informer might be one of them. What do you think?"

"Well...who knows?"

Lem looked so puzzled that Dan burst out laughing. Lem cursed under breath and strode away moving as stiffly as a first-generation robot. Behind him, the others could finally afford to join Dan in laughing. The astronautics lecture had ended completely otherwise than expected. Certainly more useful to the lecturer than to the audience.

* * * * * * *

The vibrations of the ground were quite powerful.

"What was that?"

A sequence of melodious tones filled the room. They were followed by the glimmering of the optic alarm signals.

"Nothing special. Changes in the underground passages." Teo casually displayed a dense brightly coloured network on the holo-projector. On it, he superimposed the transparent image of four spheres of different sizes which stood for the sectors where the explosions had just taken place. "Look...simultaneous blockage of three passages and one A by-passage in the operational area. Nice work."

"Yeah...but I see trouble ahead," mumbled Gil and

bent over the desk to inform the operational area about the changes.

Teo kept staring at the holo-projector.

"Gil! We've got white patches in the area. Lots of sensors there have stopped working!"

Gil stood still. Teo saw him turn halfway and guessed what was going to happen. The room was invaded by a wave of curses, as original as they were varied, in a language Gil often resorted to when they were left alone. At first he had not minded anyone hearing him, but in time, though rather late, he had taught himself common sense. Both his old and new colleagues knew that it was only his rebellious spirit that had led him to the situation of working on stable bases. Teo was new to the job but he had quickly adapted to the atmosphere. After all, not every stable-base operator could have a first class explorer for a colleague, even demoted as he was. Every situation created by something that did not "work" stirred up in Gil huge waves of protest. The astronaut then turned into a calamity. His height; his enormous mane of red hair which wildly adorned his head, his chest and arms; his powerful hollow voice; all of them gave off an irrepressible force and temperament. Now Gil was making for his colleague menacingly. Teo instinctively took refuge behind a pillar.

"Those bloody creatures," Gil said breathing deeply. "I knew from the very beginning it wouldn't work. Council of prats...! To make them fight against one another! No way. The northerners are much more numerous. More numerous and more bellicose. Unless we intervene.... Council of prats! We'll never be able to leave this planet."

"Calm down, Gil. Don't you realise how complex the situation is? Another civilisation, other beings, who the hell are we to—"

"Bullshit! Bull...shit!"

Gil's voice reached its climax again. The astronaut was striding to and fro scratching his neck nervously.

"Don't you see this war is just a stratagem of theirs? We give them robots and drills, explosives and all kinds of knowledge, and look what they're doing! Instead of using them in battle, they study them, copy them, and fortify the south of the planet. We're serving their technological progress, that's what we're doing. When they've taken everything we're willing to give them—and I see we're making the most of our good-will—they'll tell us nicely: 'We're sorry but we can't defeat them. We'll have to negotiate the recovery of that creature you call Ted. What could you give us in return? The blueprints of the anti-grav engines? Or maybe a little equipment for a Varyan biotronic ordinator? Eh?'"

"Hey, take it easy, Gil, there's no time for such speculations. You must admit they're different from us, they think differently—"

"They're different, they think differently," Gil aped Teo. "Do you want to know the truth? Our sociologists have screwed it, that's all. It's bullshit, all this attempt of ours to scientifically and technologically dope some creatures that aren't prepared to assimilate what we offer them. Some creatures that have never practised democracy. Freedom of thought? Moral codes? Social conscience as we see it? Bullshit! I may be wrong, but it's best if we have notthing to do with them. Our biggest mistake was to interfere with life on this planet.... Try to imagine the Earth three or four thousand years ago readily accepting the existence of extraterrestrial intelligent life, proved by repeated unequivocal contacts. It would have meant disaster. The history of humanity would have come to pieces."

"True, but you see, our presence here has been accepted right from the beginning. We were somehow asked to come here—"

"What? Asked to come here? By whom? By the telepathic signals of some beings more dubious than anything. Accepted—by whom? By a small group of these beings much cleverer than the average population?"

"And yet, they've managed to do so much."

"They have. A lot of things. That's exactly what worries me. And their number. Do you know how many they are?"

"No," said Teo, puzzled, not knowing what the other was getting at.

"Over fifteen billion loathsome creatures which, once you've taught something, you can be sure they won't ever forget it. Do you remember the case of the digging robots?"

Teo did not hasten to reply. Which did not mean, though, that he did not remember it. A large community of Varyans had taken over the production line of an experimental type of digging robots. The take-over was part of the so-called program of techno-scientific exchanges. Next, a delegation of Varyans had inquired about how to use the dozens of millions of unemployed individuals. The Earthlings had helped them to train and equip them for the war against the northerners.

Gil seemed to finally remember the sensors. He turned to the monitors and pressed a few keys several times.

"It's no use, Gil, the holo-projector shows it clearly. They're out of order," said Teo and saw how Gil hit hard the desk frame.

"These creatures are up to something, Teo. The explosions were too powerful and too synchronised. Show me everything you can about the area."

Teo explored the auxiliary memory bank while Gil was eagerly drumming his belt. Soon they could see a new dense intricate network of tunnels on the holo-projector.

"Look here, about five thousand kilometres from the last beacon there's a completely blocked area," said Teo enlarging the picture. "One way or another, almost everything that's caved in affects the same place. It might be just a coincidence, though."

"No, my man, it's too obvious to be a coincidence. Call the mobile base."

"Do you really think they've got time for us?" Teo waved it away.

"We'd better stick to the usual procedure: send them

a message through the exchange."

"Which will process it I don't know when. No, Teo, we've got to move fast. Don't you realise the Varyans want to isolate that area now, and not later, when we try to plant other sensors?"

"We can't do anything without an order, Gil. And there's only one good sensor left, I'm afraid."

"Listen, old man, how about planting it ourselves? We know the access way. We can always use our buggy. It's still outside, isn't it? If we plant the sensor right in the middle, we can solve the problem."

"You must be crazy!" Teo jumped from his chair. "How do you think we'll be able to go down so deep?"

"We won't have to do it. The sensor will. There's a drilling machine outside, remember? We'll show the little dears down there we can upset their plans in spite of their caved in tunnels!" said Gil and smiled.

It was a smile that froze Teo's blood. He knew it spelt trouble. The operator had seen it several times before and each time it had led to the same thing. He was in charge of this stable base all right but Gil had never seemed to care about it. Teo's chances to keep him under control were nil, he knew that too well, and he found himself hating the digging robots and their foolish habit of obeying anyone. What could he do against that giant, more than two metres high, who was now smiling broadly at the thought of another escapade? It was obvious that Gil had already worked out something.

"I don't know, Gil. It's too risky and I'm not prepared

to take any chances."

"Then I'll do it by myself," Gil yelled and hit the frame of the screen again. "Do you think I'm going to stay here and do nothing while my colleagues are in full action on the mobile bases?"

"But think of the gravity, Gil. Think of how much you're going to weigh in your suit—"

"Ha, ha," Gil burst out laughing. "Want to bet I can carry you on my back to the vehicle?"

"No," said Teo desperately. "I said I'm not going. Besides, you know the base can't be left unprotected."

"As you wish," said Gil and frowned at him. "You can help me from here instead."

* * * * * * *

In the relaxation room the silence was absolute. No noise, not even a bit of radiation penetrated the walls of the shelter. These ideal conditions were not enough for Hor, though. The Varyan's psyche had been badly shaken by the avalanche of information. Without his experience and self-control Hor would certainly have broken down. He understood that they had done it on purpose. They were probably checking his ability to absorb information. So far, he had been able to stand it, although he already felt he was wearing out.

Hor had taken advantage of the break to think of a new strategy. Obviously, there was no turning back. He and Orm were to decide the fate of the planetary conflict one way or the other. He recognised in the way Orm was conducting the negotiations his wish to avoid any misunderstandings or, worse, refusals.

The northerners' counter-offensive was going to be very powerful—there was no doubt about that. They had been putting all their resources into the war. The war came first for absolutely every member of the community. On the other hand, thanks to the Earthlings' presence in their midst, the southerners' effort did not seem to be such a burden. More than that, the machines were doing most of the work: they dug, supported the front, produced plenty of energy and goods, and created new opportunities all the time.

The door opened and in came Orm, bringing along the rustle from behind the walls.

"Come, we'll visit one of the most secret sectors here. You'll understand why my people is so optimistic and full of hope," he said. The suckers of his limbs were moving quickly over the patches of skin left free by the military outfit, nervously pinching them here and there.

He stared at the southerner waiting for his reactions. The latter's calm and immobility seemed to upset him more than his silence. Suddenly, as if reading the other's mind, Hor said.

"Why would you reveal your secrets to me?"

"Because you seem to understand the situation perfectly. You know we know enough about the cosmic beings and their role in the conflict. None of their land-ings has been a secret to us."

"True," said the southerner thoughtfully. "But their presence, apart from being an advantage, has also been a destabilising factor."

"Ah!" the northerner burst out. "Only that? Why, you southerners do know what a euphemism is! Everything's changed in your part of the planet, my dear Hor, you know that better than I do. The pace of change is so fast that it's broken loose of all control. And it's a control you'll never get again. You've destroyed the essence of our values for the chaos created by a spirit foreign to the Varyan one. Disaster will be looming over our entire civilisation until the Earthlings have left this planet for ever.... Suppose you've won the war. What's going to happen next? What will they do? What further role will they play? You don't expect you'll kindly ask them to leave and they'll do it just like that, do you? Don't forget they've built gigantic installations on large areas which filter the soil and search for those elements they so badly need. Soon they'll ask for more land and, eventually, turn the whole planet upside down. Allies? Under what conditions? At what price? And what if they decide to stay here? Think of the distance which separates them from their world."

A sombre silence ended the northerner's outburst. Hor was taking his time. At last he replied in the same even low tone.

"The Earthlings have never interfered in our conflict directly, mind you. They want nothing but to help us. They think it's preferable and necessary that the southerners should impose their will. That's why they're helping us. They're our allies."

"Allies?" Orm's scornful whistle came quickly. "They're only interested in retrieving their fellow-being who's in our hands."

"Don't forget it was you who unleashed the conflict. It was you who refused to deliver the Earthling when they first landed on our planet. Give them the prisoner and they'll leave."

"What about the war? Would the loss of so precious an ally suit you? I don't think so. You still need them. Otherwise victory is not assured."

"You northerners trust no one and nothing."

"Hor, the only thing we can handle them with is the prisoner. And the prisoner is ours. The southerners have only one solution: to accept the armistice. Then we can act together to remove the aliens for good."

Hor burst out laughing. His antennae dropped and started to throb, while his body was convulsing.

"Orm, you've completely lost your sense of reality. How do you imagine these Earthlings could be removed for good?"

"By destroying them. It's the only way for us to find our peace again."

"Fine, but how are we going to do it? You don't have a plan, do you? If you do, why don't you carry it out, you're in different camps, after all, you've admitted it yourself," Hor managed to squeeze in between two guffaws.

"Don't joke about such things, southerner. The fate of the whole planet is at stake." Orm paused, turned and waved one of his soles to Hor. "Come! I'm sure we'll find a way. As for the means of the Earthlings' removal, we've been working on them since their first landing. We have always been aware of the imminence of a confrontation. It's impossible to avoid it. We're much too different, Hor. And we must do our best to keep other intelligent beings away from our vital space."

One wall of the room disappeared leaving a wide opening instead. They stepped into it and got on a small underground vehicle that was waiting for them. The vehicle drove off through the underground network of the complex.

"Don't you think the fact that we are here now shows how necessary an armistice is?" Orm's rather weak whistle was perturbed by rhythmic noises, ever more intense, coming from below.

"One of my collaborators who set up this meeting told me the negotiations have been going on for some time."

"Then you admit the meeting was inevitable?"

"It's the Council's job to decide that. And probably your Professor's."

"The Professor no longer exists."

"What?"

"I had to remove him. He was an incompetent, a madman dominated by his own obsessive visions. He acted chaotically, all by himself. I had to do it. It's to him that you owe your big victories in our war."

"So you are now—"

"Yes, the one who can make any decision concerning

any northerner. And not only," said Orm fully enjoying the moment. Hor found it hard to sit on the bench and listen on. "Hey, take it easy. I know your decision will be decisive for the southerners, too."

"How do you know that?" Hor could hardly utter those words.

"You just mentioned a collaborator of yours. The one who told you of many things before the others learned of them."

"Yes. He's one of my best friends."

"I know. He respects you a lot, and thinks you're one of the most valuable southern assets. Very reliable, this Zeh. He's always suffered from not being able to match your honesty. He asked me to ask you to forgive him, and try to understand him. For the way in which he's tried to serve both camps, I for one consider him a true Varyan, maybe worthier than you and me.... Yes, he's a true son of the planet. Without him, we'd never have dared to face the beings coming from outer space."

Hor was choking. He felt that any moment now the extraordinary pressure of a hostile reality would crush him, make him disappear. That was exactly what he wanted, after all: to disappear from that planet as a victim of an implacable destiny.

"End of the road," Orm whistled at last in a voice that wanted to sound neutral. He started, though, not recognising it. The real end of the road was much farther, floating in the impenetrable darkness of an unforeseeable future.

* * * * * * *

The video-monitor flickered again, then the screen was flooded by an even green which showed the lack of video signal. Only the sound was as clear as before. Teo pressed the keys confusedly, trying to get the picture back. His left eyelid began to throb, which always meant trouble. He found himself interrupting Gil's tittle-tattle:

"TA-33! TA-33! BF-1! Come in, please!"

Whatever Teo had said would not have taken his colleague aback more than he did now.

"What's the matter, Teo?"

"I'm not getting any video signal!"

"So?"

"What do you mean, so? I need to see what you're doing down there."

"Hang on a minute.... It's gone."

"What's gone?"

"The portable transmitter. The batteries are dead."

"Can't you do anything about it?"

"Listen, old man. Do you think I've got time now for patching things up? I'm flying over neutral territory, remember? We'll have to do without it, that's all!"

Gil gave Teo the co-ordinates of the area and kept prattling, the only thing that betrayed his tension. He had just crossed the front line. Soon he would have to launch the robot. Although the machine was a fast digger, much depended on the hardness of the soil. It was a matter of minutes or hours. Once the hole had been made, he would put the sensor in it and leave.

"Hey, let's have a break. Stick to the same direction

for another hour or so. Then you can call me," said Teo.

"Aye, aye, old man."

Gil had accepted it too easily, it was not really in his nature. He called Teo three quarters of an hour later.

"I think I'm home, Teo. Hovering over a dry area. No sign of any activity."

"Be careful, Gil. Those creatures can come up any time. And they've got the means to knock you down."

"Listen, old man. Do you know what an explorer's good for? To take all the risks in the world, unlike people like you, who stay put and behave like smart-arses."

Teo refrained from answering back and checked the ship's position. Indeed, Gil had got there sooner than expected, and he was right above the target.

"I see you can handle things without my help pretty well. You can launch the robot now."

Gil's answer was a sullen mumble. Gil was, no doubt, a worthy man despite his whims. He knew how to make himself appreciated, if not by his bosses, then certainly by those whom he worked with. He had once admitted, while wearing their subconscious-exploring helmets which allowed them to see almost everything that lay in their minds, that Teo was a reliable good–hearted chap. Gil did not even suspect what those words had meant to Teo. They had helped him to survive those grim moments that any stable base experienced. To Gil the base was just a "lousy box" where nothing ever happened. He came from another life in which everything that did not mean action and risks was openly scorned. Maybe that was why Gil found living on a stable base such a hard burden to bear.

Teo felt he was a bit fond of this hairy giant with such unpredictable reactions. He almost loved Gil when, encroaching on orders, he ventured all by himself on a hardly possible mission that offered him something of his former life. He wished he were in his place now even though, if they did not succeed, they were certainly going to get into the most frightful trouble. He did not care about that any more: his base was no longer the place where nothing ever happened. And he owed that to Gil.

* * * * * * *

"This area is close to the front line," said Orm. "When we started building the labs we couldn't guess you'd get so far. For the time being, by several controlled explosions, we've blocked the underground entrances."

"What about the surface ones?" asked Hor.

"There are no surface ones."

"Then how did we get in?"

"By the only entrance the Earthlings' robot spies were able to find. When your troops approached, we decided to withdraw. We evacuated most of the personnel, blocked the tunnels, and waited for you. Among the few that are still here there's someone I'm pretty sure you'd love to meet."

It was not hard for Hor to guess whom Orm was talking about. He tried to curb his feelings but the northerner had already noticed his reaction and grinned.

"That's right. Sit's here. If we reach an agreement, you can take him back. He's no more use to us."

"You can't blackmail me by taking advantage of the delicate situation this great scientist's in. The fact that we happen to know each other won't influence our negotiations in any way. I'm convinced he wouldn't accept such a thing either."

Orm did not seem to be listening. He passed quickly from one room to another, and Hor had to hurry in order not to be left behind the doors which shut fast with a bang almost immediately after the northerner touched the sensors cunningly concealed in the walls. The southerner thought angrily that it would be impossible for him to cover the way back all by himself in case he needed to.

"Orm, am I to understand that the Earthling's here too?" he asked, breathing hard.

"Yes, you are. We'll evacuate him too, in a special container. He's an essential part of our plan. Sit's staying with him, concluding his research."

"I don't understand," said Hor and stopped, waiting for an explanation. Orm had to turn around. He looked a little embarrassed.

"We've conceived a program for annihilating the cosmic beings. We won't use missiles, of course— their shock deviation or absorption screens render them useless. We focused on the Earthling's structure. Sit helped us a lot there without knowing it. He told us the most efficient way to kill any form of life on their planet is to destroy the structure of the essential factor that determined its appearance."

"And what would that factor be?"

"Something banal. The liquid hydrogen oxides. Water is the environment that determines the exchanges of matter, energy, and information within the most elementary living structure—the cell structure. Any Earthling organism is made up of very diverse cells which are grouped in diverse ways. One change in the structure of the water in these organisms and death is instantaneous. All vital processes get completely blocked."

"And how do you do it? By dissociation or combination with something else?"

"No, those are chemical transformations. They'd be too complicated and, therefore, too slow. We've found another method. We change its physical state. Using radiations of a certain type, we change the molecular interaction. From liquid, this substance changes instantly into gel. In its gel state, water is no longer that miraculous environment that feeds the vital process. On the contrary, it becomes the most powerful impediment. That's our weapon, Hor."

Orm showed Hor a small metal sphere with spiral filaments. Hor examined it carefully and asked.

"Does it work?"

"Of course," Orm said and laughed when he saw the southerner pointing the gun at him. "But don't try to use it on me, it won't have any effect. There's no liquid water in our make-up that conditions a vital function.

You'll only get a few kinetic disturbances at the most."

"What's the range?"

"Well, it varies with the weather."

"So it's limited. And therefore not lethal."

"Just wait and see. We've already made quite a number of them—one for at least a hundred soldiers."

"What makes you think the Earthlings will fight themselves? They could always use their robots."

"Who will be stopped by our energy fields. You know that too well. Not having Varyans to fight for them, they'll lose. There're too many of us. When we've improved our weapon and multiplied it by the million, the Earthlings will go back to ther ship which is orbiting our planet. And there they'll experience another kind of death, slower but surer. You are surprised, aren't you?"

Orm spun his antennae in high spirits, seeing how Hor betrayed his feelings again. Hor was shocked by the northerner's aggressiveness. They had certainly chosen to fight the war their own way and had the resources to win it.

"But where did you get this idea from?" Hor finally managed to utter.

"By examining the Earthling's body, of course. Its most important element is carbon. Carbon and its unstable forms, the isotopes, to be more exact, present in all the cells and even the subcell structures. There's a fixed period for each isotope in which it changes into another element. Well, we've discovered how to shorten this period thousands and thousands of times.

Are you with me?"

It was a useless question. Hor was all ears. Under the excitement, his skin started to twist in small whirls while his antennae were beating the air restlessly.

"Now let's see what would happen if we hastened the transformation of an Earthling's carbon isotopes," Orm whispered on, waving his limbs. "It's very simple: the carbon atoms would turn into nitrogen atoms. Unfortunately, the number of carbon isotopes is quite low in an Earthling's body to endanger its integrity immediately. More than that, once dead, the degraded biological structures would be quickly removed and replaced by new ones."

"How does he do that? Does he make them himself? Can he influence those changes?"

"I don't know. What I do know is that his whole body regenerates itself plenty of times in the course of its life. We've also discovered where the information that ensures the permanent process of replacement is hidden. It's in absolutely each and every cell of the body."

"Then you can't get anywhere by accelerating the transformation of isotopes."

"We can. Because even those elementary biological structures that contain the plans for rebuilding the destroyed or modified cells include carbon atoms and, implicitly, isotopes likely to change into nitrogen. During the life of an Earthling organism, which is much shorter than ours, these structures degrade themselves irreversibly due to the ever larger number of unstable carbon atoms changed into nitrogen. Even if their number's comparatively small, it's very important because it changes the information whereby all living units of the body are renewed. The body'll keep renewing its structures but they'll be more and more imperfect because they'll be copying information which is more and more altered. Do you understand?"

"Yes," the southerner whistled thoughtfully. "It'll be like a chain reaction, ever faster, ever more devastating."

"Unlike them, our bodies are linked to a biofield and not to some poor degradable structures. We're categorically superior to these beings."

"How do you know their biofield doesn't play a similar role?"

"Sit told me that. His researches started everything. Some of the conclusions may be wrong but all in all things stand exactly as I told you. The fact is we're going to build several focalisers in various areas of the planet in order to keep under surveillance the stratospheric and cosmic space around Var. One of the reasons why we need your co-operation is to be able to set a number of focalisers in your part of the planet too. We've already finished several dozens of generators designed to excite the carbon isotopes. One of them is right here, beneath us. The moment we focus the beam of radiations on their ship, their biological time will be accelerated thousands of times faster than usual. They'll be getting old from one moment to another. They'll die before knowing what's happening to their bodies. And we'll be the masters of their ship and, if we want, the masters of their civilisation."

* * * * * * *

"OK, old man. It's digging. I'm watching it from up here. It landed exactly where it was supposed to land. I like the machinery a lot. It's moving well."

Teo felt a hump in his throat. He began to shout into the microphone.

"I've seen them before. They turn around as if trying to find a more comfortable position and all of a sudden you see they've already dug a huge hole under them. In less than a minute you see only rock thrown upwards."

"Hey, you don't have to shout. I can hear you well."

Gil kept quiet for a while. He must be very nervous, being on the watch out for the enemy and all, Teo thought.

"How's it going?" Teo was fidgety, feeling the need to talk. The walls around were like a trap to him.

"Still OK! There's a long whirl of gas and dust coming out from the hole. That's about all I can see, apart from the data on the dashboard here in the cabin."

Suddenly, Teo heard Gil swear violently.

"What happened? Did it stop?" Teo asked.

"Yeah. But it's not coming up. What can have happened?"

"I don't know."

"What do you mean, you don't know? Why isn't it coming up?"

Silence followed, marked by the same discreet, even

buzz of the engines. In front of the dashboards, Teo and Gil sensed each other's tension about to explode.

"I'm going to call it up and cancel the program."

"No, wait. Maybe it's analysing something."

"What? It's job is to dig, for God's sake!"

"I said wait!" Teo yelled. "It has special sensors for analysing the kind of obstacle it has to penetrate. Maybe that's what it's doing now, analysing. Maybe it's found something."

"Found what? I can't see anything on the screen."

Teo sighed with relief.

"Listen! If there's nothing about the type and composition of the rock, then it hasn't finished analysing. I'm quite sure it's come across another type of rock."

"You're right. I can see the data now."

"And?"

Gil replied by way of an exclamation of surprise. Teo waited patiently. He knew there was a bombshell coming. And it came.

"Hard isotropic matter. Metal alloy. Thickness, almost one metre. Elevation, minus a hundred metres. That's it!"

"Launch the sensor and leave!" Teo shouted and pulled the zip of his suit down to the belt. He was suddenly hot.

"No. The robot's not coming up and I'm not going to call it."

"Gil. Are you nuts? A few minutes ago you wanted to stop the digging and now, when everything's clear, you want to go on?"

"That's right, old man, because now I know what's down there. A danger you know is always preferable to the unknown, no matter what. That's it! If the machine thinks it can pass through, why should I be against it?"

Teo did not agree but thought better of it and swallowed his protest. He remembered how obstinate Gil could be and decided to dance to his tune for the time being.

"All right. But keep an eye on it."

"I will. From what I see, our robot's trying to show off. It's about to start melting the metal. It's already started actually. Working temperature: three thousand degrees Celsius," Gil said, and added as an afterthought: "I'll be very lucky if it gets away with it."

Teo knew the robot could do it if the conductivity of that alloy was not very high. He tried in vain to resume the dialogue. Gil had fooled him again. He felt humiliated, completely dependent on the other. Gil was obviously getting his own back on Teo's refusal to join him. He started to pace the cabin up and down. Time hung heavier than ever. It weighed on his shoulders, exhausting him.

Gil called him only a quarter of an hour later.

"It's made it!"

"What?"

"It's passing through the third level now. Elevation: minus a hundred and twenty-six metres."

"What third level? What...what about the second one?"

"Our friend went through it without stopping.

Which, at such a speed, is quite understandable."

"What speed?"

"There was an empty space under the metal barrier. Our robot fell through it like a missile," Gil laughed, sounding as if he had outrun the crisis.

"How much more do you want to let it dig?"

"Until it hits rock again. The same type as the one above the metal barrier. I can't help laughing when I think of the creatures down there seeing it. As fine a show as anyone would wish. They hardly understand what's going on and...booom!...it's gone below to entertain the others too. Old man, listen to me, and listen to me good. We've made it. There's something special down there, a sort of base, or shelter, or warehouse. I won't stop until I've planted the sensor right at the last level. Under the last level, that is."

"Do you think they won't realise what's going on?"

"They will, but not now. Now they've got no chance to do it. They must be thinking it's some kind of surprise attack. And it is in a way. What with the racket it's making and with its huge spouts, it's equal to an entire shock unit."

"It certainly is, Gil, it certainly is. Don't you think they might take it for an elevator?"

"Why not? Wait till they get the sensor; it weighs at least two tons. They won't be disappointed at all."

They kept joking until Gil announced the lowest elevation accepted: minus two hundred metres. He bade farewell to the robot, saying it had done the best job of any machine of that type. Then he launched the massive metal projectile which was able to detect and transmit any information related to the forms of energy or communication its force field was going to interact with.

"Do you think it'll resist a long time down there?" asked Teo and immediately realised the answer was not that important. To him it was more important that the operation had been successful than the benefits they were going to get from it.

"You bet," said Gil convincingly. "Long enough to give them a hard time. If they try to destroy it, the explosion will in turn destroy the whole underground complex. We've done a good job, Teo, so good I almost feel like having a look down there."

"Well...," Teo hesitated a little, then let himself be carried away by the idea. "What the hell, go ahead, try it! You can always use the mobile projector. You know how much damage light can do to the Varyans."

Ten minutes later Teo heard Gil's excited voice.

"I'm going down, Teo."

* * * * * * *

Orm was reeling out his thoughts into a sort of improvised monologue. He was looking at the ceiling as if trying to make out the intergalactic complex orbiting the planet.

"Yes...with a little bit of luck we will master everything. Provided none of them finds out anything. They mustn't know the terrible danger they're in. We can't be sure of our security unless we wipe out all the

Earthlings here. They've signed their death sentence themselves. They've discovered us, therefore they must be destroyed."

There was trouble in Orm's voice and Hor could be but amazed at what he heard.

"There is a way, though, by which they can send a message back home, warning their kind or, why not, asking for revenge. So we'll have to be quick and strike them first. And strike them hard we shall.... We've got our own plan for that. We've heard about your common project to send a probe to the Earth. What better chance to carry it out? That's why we need your co-operation, Hor, we need the co-operation of the whole south. And that's why you're here. More than half of your new Council is in permanent contact with me, did you know that? We must show them how wrong they are in looking down on us. And as long as they don't know what we've got in store for them, they're vulnerable.... Think, Hor, maybe they're not as rational as they pretend to be. What are they looking for here, at such an unimaginable distance from their home? What are they after? Exploring outer space? It doesn't wash. They themselves say the Universe has the same structure and laws everywhere. Why don't they just content themselves with their own planet, if outer space is the same wherever you turn? What do they want from us? Why don't they leave us alone? Are they possessed, goaded by some kind of madness that's pushing them farther and farther, always farther?"

"Stop, Orm," the southerner broke in, exasperated.

"You want to know what they want from us? Did you forget you're holding an Earthling prisoner? Indeed, everyone thought him dead, but now everyone knows he isn't. So you no longer have the right to keep him. You were promised an amazing reward for bringing him back to life.... If you'd been less suspicious, you could have had them on your side.... You've made a very big mistake, Orm, and that could be fatal for your people and, why not, for the whole planet.... Return the Earthling and ask them to leave. Maybe they'll do it. Thus we'll sort everything out."

"No, that would be a bigger mistake. They might leave but again they might come back."

"Then we'll fight them, without breaking our loyalty to the principles in whose name we contacted them."

"It'll be too late, I'm afraid. No, we've got the best chances now."

"What chances? The difference in evolution between them and us is huge. And your weapons...how can you be so sure they'll work? You're too self-confident, Orm. You're too sure of our co-operation."

"I am sure because this planet must truly belong to us. Wake up, Hor, before it's too late, before everything gets out of our control. You want to know if our weapons will work? All right...you'll see the first gelled victim in a minute."

"What victim? Whom do you have in mind?" Hor stepped forward waving his antennae vigorously.

"The Earthling. You can see what's left of him with your own eyes."

"Now I get it," Hor whistled and smacked his suckers rhythmically. "You never wanted to return him! Well, I'll never accept to be an ally of yours."

"You'll have to," Orm shouted rushing at Hor. "It's too late to change anything now."

"That's not true," Hor replied.

His limbs rose at lightning speed like a fan and rushed to immobilise the other's. Orm, though, was quick enough to stick his suckers to Hor's soles. The southerner grabbed his antennae and pulled them hard but to no effect. Extraordinary tension rose in one of his soles which started to turn around. Orm's limbs had stuck hard to it, trying to put Hor down. Hor realised that he was about to collapse. He used his last strength to catch hold of his opponent's antennae and, before falling, he kicked the northerner. Orm lost his balance and fell down at the same time as Hor did. They rolled about on the floor until Orm managed to stay above and press Hor with his heavier body. Hor's limbs were, however, free and he put them round Orm's neck and started to squeeze it desperately. The northerner's eyes grew bigger and bigger and, just when Hor wondered how much longer he was supposed to squeeze it like that, he felt Orm's weight lighten and his limbs fall on the floor scattering their suckers all over the place. It was only when the last of them stopped trembling that he let Orm go.

After lying there for a while, Hor stood up slowly, leaning against the wall. He looked at Orm. He was dead. He tried to remember when he had first thought of killing him. Orm had overlooked that possibility and there he was now, all dead and gone. But his war machine was still intact and so were his plans, his projects. The others were undoubtedly going to carry his orders out as soon as they heard about Orm's death.

All was not lost if he managed to inform his own people about it, Hor thought. He had to hurry. He had to find Sit. A muffled noise coming from above strengthened his conviction that the base had not been evacuated completely. He tried to open several doors but all of them were blocked solid, ready to resist a siege.

The noise was getting more and more powerful. Hor stood still: since he had entered the northern area it was the first time he heard something like that. He felt how fear heated his skin. He was trapped there, far from any chance of escape. He heard the noise drawing closer and closer. Obviously, it was coming down towards him. And it kept changing its tone: sometimes sharp, sometimes dull, drowning for a moment, to rise haltingly again.

Hor had no other choice but to wait for that thing to reach him. But first he had to get rid of Orm's body. He hid it behind some thick pipes, then came to the middle of the room and sat down. Strange, the fear had disappeared giving way to inexplicable curiosity. He felt the source of that terrible noise would turn up soon.

Suddenly, the air around him started to vibrate. Soon the vibrations turned into shock waves, shattering everything that was fragile in the room. Then hell broke out. The ceiling and supporting pillars began to tremble in unison under what seemed to be enormous pressure. Two pillars behind Hor yielded with a dry crack. The sound waves became unbearable. Hor felt his body split into pieces that were pulsating in an unnatural resonance.

The walls and the floor were shaking violently. The ceiling swelled above the broken pillars and a few moments later it was as if it shattered, making way for a huge spinning body whose terrifying roar deafened Hor. Before losing his consciousness, Hor was showered by a rain of debris and a light that blinded him and burned portions of his exposed skin.

After a while, Hor recovered. He could not say how long he had been lying in that confused state, surrounded by rubble and metal splinters. When he was finally able to brush his antennae, fanning them cautiously, the first thing he noticed was a huge round hole yawning in the floor. He crawled to its edge and looked up. He saw another hole, as big as the one next to him, which had been made through two levels of the underground complex and numerous rock layers up right to the surface where everything ended in light. He glimpsed a patch of dark blue sky with two reddish spots which were twinkling mysteriously.

He lay motionless for a moment. Those stars reminded him of something...something very important to him. His thoughts were moving slowly through the dull pain that was assaulting his senses, overwhelming him. What could those stars mean to him? Infinite space, which few Varyans could think of without risking inhibition? Certainly, there was nothing on Var that could be linked to that mysterious brilliance he felt attracted to as if it were the most important thing in the whole of Nature. And all of a sudden he remembered. A triumphant smile blossomed on his transfigured face.

"The Earthlings!"

* * * * * * *

"Teo, can you read me?"

"Yeah, it's OK."

"I think I've reached the third level. Not the shadow of a ghost, but I'm not surprised. One must be sick to stand up to the machine's devastating whirl. Just remains of installations I can't make anything of. Nothing's normal here. Nothing I'm familiar with, that is. And the colours, Teo. They're the strangest blends of colours I've ever seen."

"Forget that. Better see you won't be attacked. There's no time for admiring interior decorations."

"Stop patronising me, will you? Isn't that why I've gone down? To look around a bit, enjoy the show? I won't get another opportunity, I'm sure. Anyway, there're no Varyans around here. Not even corpses."

"Maybe that's just a deserted base."

"Maybe," said Gil hesitatingly. "But I don't think so. Their attempt to hide it was too obvious. I'll go farther down."

"Take good care. You never know."

"I'm approaching the last level, Teo," said Gil after a while. "The sensor's right below me, I can see it perfectly. It went through the digging machine."

"Hey, Gil, I can hardly hear you at all. Come back!"

Then Teo started to count the minutes and think of some way of helping Gil, just in case: to go down there himself using the only buggy left on the base; to alert the intergalactic complex which was in stationary orbit somewhere above the south pole of the planet—it was only the deal they had made for Teo not to report anything before the end of the operation that prevented him from doing it.

If he came to think of it, their operation was in many ways above reproach, except for the fact that they had interfered rather brutally in the conflict between the north and the south. Not that the astronauts' declared non-intervention attitude had not been compromised several times before, without the Council members making a problem out of it.

The Council had other things to worry about now. Ted was still in the northerners' hands. There were no more telepathic messages coming from him. More and more councillors were inclined to direct, drastic action. The Varyans hesitated between the Earthlings staying neutral and decisively participating in the conflict. Their fear of the Earthlings was very much there, although they managed to hide it quite well. The relations between the Varyans and the Earthlings had become confused, either party considering itself more disadvantaged than the other. If only the biotronic ordinator were functioning, how quickly it would sort everything out. Teo did not like all those Varyans visiting the intergalactic complex, absorbing scientific and technological information at an unimaginable speed, trying to profit as much as possible from the presence of men on their planet. He feared that, sooner or later, unless they left Var, the astronauts were going to pay for it.

After exactly one hour and a half, Teo heard Gil's voice again.

"Teo, old man, can you hear me?"

"Yes. What happened? Where are you?"

"On the ground. You know whom I've got next to me? A native. He was on the last level, lost among all sorts of installations. Looks quite self-confident, though I've somewhat confused him with the projector. Seems very interested in me. And when I think I considered them a bunch of cowards. He didn't run away. On the contrary. He set about smearing all sorts of things on the wall. He drew me twice, then he drew himself and a sort of autonomous flight set similar to mine. After I got fed up with his stories, I grabbed him and came up with him. Now he's whistling like a siren and struggling like mad."

"Keep him covered, Gil. Light hurts him."

"He's taken care of that himself. Knows how to save his skin."

"Let me hear him," said Teo and pressed a few keys.

A strangely modulated whistle rushed into the cabin. Teo coupled the filters and saw that the gauges showed a range that went well beyond the human audio one. Then an idea struck him.

"Gil, did you know every stable base is equipped with a translator?"

"Are you joking?"

"No, I mean it. Try to tell him he'll be understood. You've got three minutes to do it."

Teo ran excitedly through the long rows of codes until he found what he was looking for. He checked it quickly and sighed with relief. The cassette was there. He took it out and glanced at it. Then he put it in the ordinator and shouted.

"Gil, forget all the explanations. Shove the receiver in front of his mouth and let him whistle."

"I can't. I've got some problems. First, the receiver's coupled to my helmet. Then, I don't know where his mouth is. He's wrapped up in some sort of fabric and hopping about. He can't have all his marbles, can he?"

"Come on, Gil, don't be ridiculous! Find something. I know you can."

During the next few minutes Teo could hear a lot of swear words and a hubbub of strident whistles that almost broke his eardrums. At last he heard Gil gasp and shout.

"OK! I've got him safe in my arms! Turn it on!"

The cabin resounded with the shouts and whistles of the two, locked in an embrace equally embarrassing for both of them. Teo could not take his eyes off the screen. He did not even blink for a while. Then, when he remembered Gil was waiting for his reply, he exclaimed.

"Gil, it's fantastic. Absolutely fantastic. Listen!

I haven't got time to tell you everything. Just let the Varyan down and go back, both of you, to where you found him. He'll realise you've understood him and will take you to something that must look like a container. That's where Ted is. Do you get it? And don't let the Varyan go. He's Ted's only chance now."

"All right, old man. Listen! I'll try to bring the container up. At any price. You get in touch with anyone you can. I feel we've made it. Stay tuned. I'm off!"

Suddenly both Gil's voice and the whistles disappeared. Teo fell into his armchair, exhausted. Without a doubt, he was experiencing the tensest moments in the entire expedition. He used the priority channels to send the information and, after he received the confirmation of the transmission, he remained in front of the video-monitor not caring about anyone and anything else. His extremely jangled nerves were taking care of themselves. This made Teo a lucid man but lacking any kind of desire however small, except only to fall soundly asleep. He suspected the overtax inhibitor in his belt was the cause of it but he did not disconnect it. He liked it that way.

The monitor's signal found him exactly like that three hours later. He could see the hole in the ground surrounded by broken rock. Around them there were a lot of astronauts—Ted's team. Somewhere aside, there was Gil next to two indistinct small shapes covered by a kind of flexible bell. One of them was moving. Teo did not wonder why Gil had two natives now instead of one. He must have found the other while trying to retrieve Ted.

He could also see the container. It looked rather small and fragile. Was Ted really in there? Then Gil's face appeared on the screen.

"Hi there, old man. How's it going?"

Teo could not believe his eyes. Gil's hair was grey at the temples and he had a slight bent in the shoulders. He looked at least fifteen or twenty years older than he had been a few hours ago!

* * * * * * *

"Well?"

"Well what? I'm back in business, that's all," said Gil a little embarrassed, unwilling to show his joy. He and Teo were going their separate ways, after all.

"Pity. I'd got used to you and your funny habits, which is something not everyone can brag about. But I'm glad you got your old job back. You did show them men like you are always in need."

These pioneers had always been different from the other astronauts. For one thing, they were not allowed to get involved too long in the basic projects lest their loss might jeopardise the entire expedition. They were the only people whose security was not guaranteed by the laws governing the operations in outer space. In some cases, they could even be withdrawn from the incidence of the first law of robotics, something unimaginable for a man under ordinary circumstances. Pioneers had to take complex tests continually, and special psychological and physical training. They enjoyed autonomy aboard any spaceship and any attempt to make them blindly submit to the rules was met with protests and indignation. Their presence became indispensable when the hostility of outer space and the unknown had to be overcome. It was then that life became worth living for them. The history of outer space exploration was full of their names but, unfortunately, those times were gone now. The volunteers, fewer and fewer, were being replaced by sophisticated robots. There were very few occasions when it was decided that only a man could fulfill a difficult mission.

"One question, Gil, before you go. How many years did they give you for the irradiation you got down there?"

"About twelve. They'll make the final decision in the following months. The whole medical team of the complex checked me up. I'm kind of fed up with them, you know."

"I'm really sorry this operation's taken so many years of your life. I wouldn't have agreed to your going down there if I'd known that."

"It's all right," said Gil and a playful light showed in his eyes. "I've got some compensations in return. A few priorities for the more difficult missions, which is neither here nor there."

Teo seemed to hesitate, Then he asked the question that was bothering him.

"Tell me, Gil, do you think we've lost the battle with Var?"

"Are you joking? We were informed of the north-erners' aggressive intentions and put ourselves out of their range of action, that's all. You don't mean to say our withdrawal looks like a flight, do you?"

Teo nodded.

"Could be. If we hadn't done it, we could've got into big muddle, all of us. Do you know what impressed our Council most? Ted's state, of course, and my meta-morphosis. I'll never forget the councillors' faces when they unanimously decided that we all leave the planet. Then the stunning statement coming from the Varyan I found in that underground lab. It was probably the first and last honest statement from a native of Var. And the probe they sent to Earth. That was, I think, our biggest mistake. Some of the councillors have already paid dearly for it. Even Dan's authority's been shattered. More of it will come out when we've left this galaxy, anyway."

"Why don't they reveal everything now?"

"Because some lab people still need the Varyans. Especially Sit, the one who accompanied Ted here."

"And the probe? What happened to it?"

"A sort of mixed commission, made up of north-erners and southerners, apparently proposed that all parties involved forget the conflict for a while and make the launch of the probe the first step towards reconciliation. So every party put their own message in the probe. Well, what do you think the northerners put in there?"

"...?"

"A bomb! Once it reached its destination, the probe was supposed to kill all life on Earth."

"Impossible! They couldn't make such a terrible bomb."

"Teo, did you forget we left Var in a great hurry some time ago?"

"Yes, but...."

"We found that out. Just on time. It seems the initiator was one of the Varyans I came across, the dead one. Well, just before the launching, we asked the commission to improve the flight program and offered to give them a helping hand in the process. You know Lem, don't you?"

"The pilot?"

"Yes. He came up with a crazy idea which in the end turned out for the best. First, he checked to see if the bomb was just cosmic dust in the absorption nozzles of the tachyons—a false alarm, that is," Gil added when he saw confusion on Teo's face.

"And?"

"It wasn't. Lem found a big ball of anti-matter instead, plus the installation that kept it stable—some strange energetic fields that keep it away from the probe walls. Did you know the Varyans are experts in sub-quantum physics?"

"No. Go on."

"Originally, the first stage of the probe flight was to be a leap into hyperspace, as we had on our way to Var; then the probe would've had a normal glide along the gravitational lines. An exact reconstruction of our own flight, but the other way round."

"Then Earth would've been saved anyhow. We didn't take off from Earth in the first place."

"That's one thing the Varyans never knew. Well, Lem suggested some changes in the flight program that were meant to speed the flight up. The Varyans accepted them almost instantly, happy that the probe could reach the destination much faster. If they hadn't, we'd have had to besiege Var and not let the probe take off. Its interception and destruction after the launching were next to impossible."

"What changes did Lem suggest that sounded so convincing to the Varyans?"

"That I don't know. We'll have to wait for the Council's full report. What I know for sure is that they accepted Lem's suggestion to make the second stage of the flight a hyperspace leap too. But they didn't know that this would involve a change in time's arrow. And they didn't know another thing either: the probe's destination was not the third planet of our solar system but the fifth one—Phaeton! Then the probe took off."

"But Phaeton's a transit station, with quite a lot of people and robots working there. What happened to them? Did the Council accept their loss so easily?"

"There was no loss. Just a cosmic cataclysm, that's all."

Teo was sure now that Gil was up to his usual tricks. He played the innocent and asked naively.

"What do you mean 'just a cosmic cataclysm'?"

"Well, this second leap, made without its necessary

energy being provided, loaded the probe with some sort of energetic deficit compared to which the Varyan bomb was nothing."

"I don't get it, Gil."

"It's like sending a container by space-mail. If you don't pay for it, they'll charge the addressee."

"I see," said Teo trying to sound convincing.

"In plain words, the probe slowed down until it reached sub-light speed and it did so in the proximity of Phaeton. That's where the cosmic cataclysm unleashed as a result of an immense energetic absorption. Phaeton couldn't have resisted. The other planets may have been affected too. As I said, we haven't got anyone on our consciences. Maybe only ourselves. Strange, isn't it?"

Gil let his heavy hand fall on Teo's shoulder.

"No, I'm not raving. Not yet," he whispered. "It's been fifteen thousand Earth years since we left our planet. Who can promise us that, once we've gone back to Earth, we won't find another civilisation knowing us only by some vestiges that have withstood the merciless passage of time. But what's the use of worrying about it? What's the use of worrying about Phaeton being there only as an asteroid belt on who knows what solar orbit? And Var, the planet which sooner or later will cease to exist? Listen to me, old man! These questions don't do anyone any good. I'd better be going, before I'm no longer responsible for what I think," said Gil laughing unnaturally and left with long, measured steps.

PART III

The creation of wealth is certainly not to be despised, but in the long run the only human activities really worthwhile are the search for knowledge and the creation of beauty.
Arthur C. Clarke

No, it was not just an impression. The deep dark his eyes had vainly been delving into faded away like a net whose meshes get bigger and bigger, embroidering on the texture of nothingness little dots of pale red, slowly broadening, joining, invading his sockets.

Calmly, completely detached, as if the sight of those images were the most natural thing possible, Ted was waiting. He had learned that a long time ago. It was, in fact, the only thing he could do in his paradoxical state whose beginning he could not even guess in the distant past. This state seemed sufficient in itself to decide his reactions. Absolute immobility had become something natural, no longer torturing him. Even the taste of resignation had stayed somewhere behind, buried in the mist of some feelings that seemed to belong to other times or maybe to another being.

However, the calm and waiting that Ted thought

had enveloped him showed signs of drawing to an end. On that strangely transparent vivid red that was everywhere, Ted suddenly discovered a small dark dot. The rugged dot might have been unnoticed if its unruly, lively dance had not drawn his attention, puzzling him. Its unexpected route was drawing imaginary lines, sometimes long, sometimes short, forming various angles to go on with volutes and spirals that, for a few moments, curiously brought the dot back to its original position. Then everything started all over again, in other directions, a spontaneous paradoxical mixture that pulled Ted out of his torpor. *There* was an opportunity for him to notice, to perceive a movement of his own senses. This was happening for the first time since...since when, really? The astronaut was experiencing a revelation that, for a second, upset him.

It then turned into a challenge and Ted found himself imperceptibly carried away by the game of careful observations and deductions belonging to simple, rather intuitive logic. He tried harder to see what it was all about. Strange, none of the dot's unpredictable trajectories brought it closer to him. And yet it looked so familiar to him. What tricks was his imagination playing on him? Was he on the threshold of another nightmare? While looking feverishly for the answer, he was trying to keep calm and lucid, the only way he could win the competition between reason and the subconscious for he himself was the stake. He kept repeating to himself, stubbornly, clinging on to the little ground he had gained: It's real, it's real, I'm lucid,

I see a dot in motion, I know it, it's closely linked to my past, oh, my memory, my memory. And the dot was there, daring him, annoying him, driving him crazy with its incursions into the red ocean to turn back sharply, always at the same speed, always with the same precision.

Then Ted remembered. In a flash that unfettered his body from its numbness, ending its inertia and oblivion. That dot.... It was on his left eye, somewhere at the edge of the pupil. He felt it whenever he shut his eyes and saw through the eyelids the light outside. Now he thought it was one of those times but, when he opened his eyes with a slight tremor, he saw in amazement that the light was not red at all but white, with bluish shades. Above him, he saw the luminous ceiling characteristic of all medical offices in the intergalactic complex. He smiled and sighed with relief. He realised the nightmare was finally over. He was home again.

The pleasant sound of an acoustic sensor made Eva start. She glanced around and saw it next to Ted's bed. Ted looked motionless in spite of the sensor's reaction. Worried, she came up to the astronaut, looked at him and, in the following moment, their eyes met. The woman bent over and kissed him.

"Try not to move, my darling," she whispered with tears in her eyes, while her hands were looking for his in clumsy haste. "Oh, Ted, my darling Ted, I missed you so much," she added and kissed him again. Then she turned full of hope to the head of the health department who had just come in.

"He's finally recovered," he said in a low but vigorous voice, while examining Ted. "He moved a little, and that's the best sign we can get. He'll have to control all his movements, though. I think it'll take him some time before he's himself again."

As if he wanted to answer, Ted opened his mouth and uttered a few inarticulate sounds. He stopped soon, however, apparently embarrassed by his performance.

"Well, well," exclaimed the doctor. "Look at him! He wants to speak!"

With tears still running down her cheeks, Eva laughed.

"I'll stay here and teach him how to move, to walk, to eat, just as we both taught Tim. Right, darling?"

At last, Ted managed to grin at her, then he opened his mouth, thought better of it, and just nodded several times.

Attracted by the noise, other members of the medical personnel appeared in the room, as well as astronauts belonging to other services. Soon the room was packed with people. They all passed by Ted, not being able to tear their eyes away from him, as if he were a being from another world, greeted him, received his nod and movement of the hands, but forgot to leave. They uttered exclamations of wonder and joy, threw in a joke, or just laughed. After a while, someone suggested calling Dan and Mag and telling them to come over to see the miracle. Then, at the doctor's insistence, they left.

* * * * * * *

Ted spoke the first words that very day. The doctor had to put him to sleep, though, as he was tempted to speak and move all the time. The next day, he started to walk, his first wish being to go to the navigator's quarter. Eva offered to accompany him.

"You're going to get a shock there," she said.

"What kind of shock?"

"The navigators have a new companion."

Ted stood still. Then he said.

"I don't want to see him, at least not now. We'd better see Dan first."

"You don't want to see whom?"

"The alien. I knew he was here, on the ship. That's why, before seeing you, I thought I was still on that planet."

"But how did you know it?"

"It's an odd sensation," said Ted hesitatingly. "Like a permanent contact between us."

"Probably because of those plants you sent us. Mag's got a lot of them now in her lab."

"Maybe. It's a very complex feeling that I've never experienced before. Do you remember how Tim clung to me when you brought him to my bed? I thought we were one and the same, I thought we were merging. It almost frightened me."

"What about *me*?" Eva smiled somehow bitterly. Her voice was changed, anxious and reproachful.

"Take it easy, darling. What I feel for you is unique; you shouldn't worry about that. What I meant to say was that there's a kind of telepathic link between us.

We seem to communicate directly with each other."

"Funny," the woman decided. "Very funny. I understand it perfectly when it comes to Tim, but that creature's too much for me. Well, here we are. Dan's office. Let's see what *he* thinks of it."

"It's natural," Dan said. "From certain points of view, the Varyan is very close to you. He is the author of the program for the reconstruction of your organism, piece by piece—an extraordinary achievement. And he decodes a field that a certain part of your brain sends and defines you exactly."

"That's probably how they contacted me in the first place," said Ted.

"My dear Ted, it is he who contacted you. He made a number of experiments on you and, by using the fields he controls, he brought you back to life. Someone on Var telepathically contacted the plant you sent us and told it the news. Tim perceived the message, passed it on to Eva, Eva passed it on to Mag, and thus we decided to come and rescue you. The biotronic brain detected with its high sensitivity—which almost drove it crazy—the plant's signals and thought them an alarm call. In the end, it was the ordinator that played the main role in the operation: it ran hundreds of tests, analyses, experiments, you name it. And, the most important thing, it became active again."

"What did you find on the planet?" Ted's face was all curiosity.

"First we detected someone's attempts to contact us. He told us that you were alive and could be retrieved but that we couldn't do it without getting involved in an internal conflict going on that planet. There were two groups at war there, one standing for social and scientific progress, the other for exploitation and spiritual darkness. The progressive one was in an absolute minority, without any chance of survival. It was its members that contacted us, thanks to a program they had perfected, starting from studying you. To save you, we ordered the central ordinator to overlook the fundamental law of alien contact. The ordinator refused to comply so we had to decide for ourselves how to deal with the aliens. In the meantime, the creatures providing the field through which they could contact us began to disappear. They were the victims of a program of systematic destruction of their race, initiated by the other group of intelligent beings."

"What happened next?" asked Ted eagerly.

"We intervened. There was no other option. We influenced the evolution of the conflict, providing the progressive group with the know-how necessary for winning the war," said Dan and paused as if looking for the right words.

"And how did I get back to the ship?"

"With the help of Sit and your colleague, Gil. It was something incredible."

"Was I alive or dead at the time?"

"It's hard to say. It seems you were dead and then revived several times. I'll leave to Sit to explain that to you. I think that, after all that you've passed through, no one can know for sure when exactly someone can be declared dead. The Varyans' opinion seems to be the right one. They say death starts when the individual can no longer regenerate the energetic matrix of his own bio-field. This opinion gave much food for thought to many of us, especially to Mag, who started dreaming of preserving human brains while securing the bio-field over a long period of time. You'll be surprised to know she's already found a volunteer for such an experiment on this very ship."

"Who's that?"

"Olf, former captain of the intergalactic complex."

"Olf?" Ted burst out with a shout of surprise. "Of all the people...."

"Yes. And you'll be all the more surprised to know what his last proposal was. Although he made a lot of mistakes, Olf proved in the end he was worthier than we thought. He suggested the command of the ship be given to a man and not to the biotronic brain. An ordinator will be an ordinator, he said, and it'll never fit our own image of a leader, the integrator of working and affective relations."

"OK, OK, but there's one thing I don't understand," said Ted. "A human captain, no matter how good, can't help making mistakes. Then why choose him when, during an expedition, any mistake can be fatal?"

"Well," Dan replied, a little taken aback, "Olf gave all the councillors copies of a thorough study which pointed to the necessity of keeping the biotronic ordinator as the only acceptable leader with a difference: a leader who was virtually a member of the crew! In other words, an android. This android had to resemble man so much that everyone should take it and its behaviour for granted."

"But such experiments are no news! The idea was given up a long time ago. The psychological barrier is impossible to break."

"We thought so too, but we were wrong. Olf studied the ordinator's decisional behaviour and realised the neuronal cells had endowed the machine with new qualities and, therefore, a personality in the true sense of the word."

"So you...."

"Yes. The ordinator itself agreed to design its 'incarnation' which, I must admit, is almost perfect. For several days we were all very excited about it."

"You mean that...," Ted trailed off looking at Eva in astonishment. "And you didn't tell me anything."

"She wanted to spare you the shock of meeting him too soon. She just wanted me to prepare you for the event. Now that I've put you in the picture, you can meet him any time."

"You do refer to it as if it were an ordinary astronaut," Ted mumbled, not being able to believe what he heard.

"He does look ordinary, you'll see. His face is a synthesis of all our faces. And so are his mimicry, gestures, behaviour, tics, and voice. Studying our reactions carefully he designed himself a social intelligence which he grafted on a very complex human psyche, and so we found ourselves in front of an absolutely remarkable creature."

"What was your first reaction when you saw him?"

"It was an almost normal reaction. I was somehow prepared for it. Actually, his body differs in only one way from ours: it has its brain elsewhere, in the central module of the complex; as for his head, it contains the command and transmission relays to the bio-tronic brain and its neuronal cells."

"All right, but what did you feel when you looked him in the eyes for the first time?" Ted's voice was strident, seeming to beg for a straight answer.

"I don't know for sure," Dan grumbled. "I had the feeling I was looking at the spaceship itself. I felt the urge to ask him if the vacuum outside made him cold but I lacked the courage.... Who knows, I might ask him that some day. I found it extraordinary to see him there, in front of me, to see how he looked into my eyes, how he smiled affably and stretched out a warm, firm hand, saying in a pleasant voice, 'My name is Or-Bi. You must be Dan, mustn't you?' Well, it's impossible to describe what I really felt. You'll have to live through the experience yourself."

"I remember sitting at my console when he entered the lab and introduced himself," Eva said. "He asked us to react normally so that he wouldn't feel embarrassed. There were only women there, five or six I think, and we were all looking at him agape. Then he told us a joke and we all burst out laughing foolishly, almost hysterically. Then," she swallowed hard, "it happened. He went straight to a panel and asked a colleague about the use of some transparent lids, the kind that protects tests against accidental orders. While the poor woman was trying hard to answer, the captain, that is the android, caught his finger in a slot. He started, looked at his finger from which a thin line of blood was tricking out and said, 'My, my. Here I am, the victim of a small accident. Does any of you know how to do a haemostasis?' But we were flabbergasted, staring at the little drops of blood dripping from his finger and forming a thin dark track on the anti-static texture of the air-collector. Then he added, 'It's all right, I'll use the emergency unit. I know it must be somewhere around here. Eva, will you take me there, please?' I nodded and we both left the lab. I was so stiff that, if someone had seen us, they would have taken me for the robot and him for the human being. Soon I realised he had known all the time where the emergency unit was. While he was placing the bio-dressing on his finger, he asked me about you, Ted, how long it would take you to wake up. I said I didn't know for sure, no one could say that. Then he said something about being patient, thanked me and left." Seeing that no one said anything, Eva asked: "Ted, what do you make of it?" But Ted kept silent, so she added: "I think Or-Bi is a fantastic chap!"

"Well," Ted said as if to himself. "Where does this name come from—this Or-Bi?"

"That was Olf's wish. It comes from 'ordinator' and 'bio-tronic'."

"Tell me," said Ted. "Did Or-Bi get in touch with

Sit?"

Dan and Eva exchanged an inquiring look. Then they shrugged their shoulders helplessly.

"Besides helping me out, has Sit been of any other use?"

"It was Sit that found the cause of the biotronic brain's misbehaviour," said Eva. "In a way, he became the computer's personal doctor. Thanks to him, the ordinator found its own self again. He's very nice, this Sit. Assimilates everything very quickly and is extremely curious."

"Do you let him walk about the ship?"

"Yes," answered Dan. "But he finds it hard to adapt himself to the light. At first we feared he might get infested with the micro-organisms here, but it seems he's immune to them. On the other hand, we can't get anything from him because of the surplus of oxygen."

"How does he feed himself?"

"He absorbs a lot of the electromagnetic radiation from all the visible and ultraviolet range and, because of that, he's most of the time in a state similar to our intoxication with oxygen or drugs. In a fit of sincerity, he told us he could hardly help multiplying himself."

"Dan," said Ted, "I'd like to meet him. It's very important to me."

"You're right. You owe him so much," said Eva.

"OK," said Dan. "Let's go and see him."

* * * * * * *

Ted ignored the explosive joy of Lem and his assistant at seeing him and slowly approached Sit who was leaning against a panel, soles pushed sideways, breathing tube hanging along his body. His enormous eyes were shaded by long rows of almost immobile antennae and fixed the newcomer. Ted was fascinated. He stopped a few steps away. His eyelids closed and the astronaut passed into complete immobility. The only sign of life was his breathing, panting, hard. The two of them remained like that, one facing the other.

Everyone retreated discreetly to the big windows on the observation wall. That was where they always ended up, admiring the multitude of stars. It was by looking at them that they realised how much space they had covered. And the strange music that seemed to be coming from them.... They had detected this by mistake, while using an ordinary decoding program for the recording of the brilliance of the big stars—those stars were going to interact with the gravitational field modulators.

Some of the astronauts wore instead of ear-rings micro-translators linked directly to the radio-wave source which was coupled with the decoder. They had become true fans of this kind of music, forgetting the ordinary music programs of the ship. Some thought there was a composer behind those sounds, although the general conclusion was that the music was just a matter of chance. More than that, some had discovered surfaces and volumes in ceaseless motion that they said influenced the gravitational shields—hence the music. They were about to combine sounds and images considering the former audio-signals of the latter. Looking at the immensity beyond the windows, they were probably thinking of the sensation their findings would cause.

After a long while, a slight noise coming from behind drew their attention. Sit was coming up to them, waving his antennae jovially. He said through the air-filter box.

"Your colleague's fallen asleep. That's the effect of the telepathic flux, no doubt. That was unusual to me too, to meet this human being under normal circumstances, a human being who, in a way, is my creation, isn't he? I must admit that if I hadn't had the inspiration to lean against that panel, I'd have collapsed and he'd have burst out laughing just as you yourselves have done too, several times by now." Seeing the others smile, Sit added: "I even think I care for this Earthling, although he's ugly, just like you all. But I won't say it out loud while he's around until I'm sure he feels the same about me."

"Of course," said one if the astronauts. "But we hope you'll invite us to be present when you make your declaration of love to him. We'll record it as a document of utmost importance in the history of our relations with the Varyans."

A general guffaw resounded in the room.

"You fools! I can make up thousands of jokes about the way you look like. The fact I've got no one to tell them to is a real torture for me."

Then Sit turned to Lem and said.

"Can we resume our discussion?" Lem nodded and Sit continued: "You said anti-gravitational engines allow the alteration of space and time lines facilitating high speeds. My question is: how high can these speeds be?"

"Thousands of times higher than the speed of light. And when it comes to hyperspace leaps, the speed of light becomes the lowest speed possible."

"How come? I for one knew that was the highest speed possible," Sit exclaimed, visibly impressed. "How can you operate a ship at such speeds?"

"By means of machines that think and act very fast. They all make up the nervous system of the ship. Of this ship, for instance. It's only with this kind of equipment that we can reach our objective."

"That's fantastic. And what is this objective?" Sit's overexcitement made his antennae move restlessly in all directions.

"It's the top priority objective, embedded into the biotronic brain by design, on Earth. The brain can never give it up. Under certain circumstances, however, if temporary interests call for it and are well grounded, the ship *can* change its course. From this point of view, our return to Var can be seen as an exceptional event."

"OK, but what *is* the objective?"

"Reaching some very dense stellar formations, the biggest concentrations of matter and energy in the Universe. We call them quasars. We're looking for a source of energy. We want to make a breach in the universe. For this we need a quasar, to couple it with a black hole. The most difficult courses we had were in our own galaxy as well as in yours. They are, in fact, the only ones we really covered."

"What do you mean?"

"That our course crosses the intergalactic space. Crossing a galaxy involves low speeds, therefore wasted time, to say nothing of obstacles of all kinds. Intergalactic spaces are much vaster. They're two or three times bigger than the galaxies. If you want to reach your objective, you mustn't cross any agglomeration of stars."

"Then how did you get to Var?"

"By mistake. Your galaxy is perpendicular to our course. We had to choose between avoiding and crossing it. Avoiding it would have taken too much time. So we crossed it and thus came across your civilisation. But we won't make the same mistake again. There were too many weird things that happened to us: the ordinator got out of control, Ted's accident on your planet, a number of incredible coincidences...which are no longer called coincidences."

"How many galaxies do you think you'll leave behind?"

"Somewhere between fifteen and eighteen. Which will cover almost three billion light-years. We are only half-way."

"Three bill...."

Sit did not manage to repeat the whole number because the shock cast him on to the floor.

"I want to go back to Var!" he said after a while.

"To Var? Well, my dear fellow," Dan put in smiling, "those energy formations we're heading for are, among other things, time-space nodules of the Universe. In other words, the fundamental structure of outer space is made of them. You'll have to accompany us there. We need you in our struggle with nothingness. For the triumph of life and intelligence in the Universe."

Dan turned to the large windows and waved at the stars.

* * * * * * *

Dan and Sit were in the level B3 central square all by themselves.

"All right," said the alien. "What do you want to know?"

"First, I'd like to know what your attitude towards outer space is. You're the one and only Varyan to have left his planet of his own accord."

Sit's answer did not come at once. Dan used the pause to observe his body language. He had learned how to guess the Varyans' moods after their bodies' reactions. Their body language was very expressive and it seemed they used it deliberately to facilitate their communication with the astronauts. Sometimes the depth of such moods far surpassed the translator's dry, formal language. The Varyans seemed to be very emotional, sensitive, and different from what their appearance suggested at first sight. To accept their presence, to make them less repulsive, the Earthlings had to associate them with something familiar. Now, for instance, Dan associated Sit with an old tree trunk which had several gnarls for branches, each ending in a flat, somewhat oval, leaf. The 'trunk' had a deeply furrowed bark adorned with a thick weave of seaweed instead of a crown. For roots, it had two naturally, evenly eroded limestone formations which made it stable and, at the same time, enabled it to move.

Dan's fantasising was interrupted by the translator's hollow voice.

"At first I didn't want to do it. You know that, to a Varyan, leaving the underground can be fatal. One look at the sky equals psychic blockage. The sky has nothing to do with our underground life."

"Well, in our case the sky's always attracted us, making us dream of flying, and leaving the planet behind."

"What about your oceans? I know you've conquered them quite recently, despite your sophisticated technology. You shouldn't wonder why we've never wanted to fly as long as you yourselves found it so hard to conquer your deep waters. I think it's normal for every civilisation to first try and master the environment that made its appearance possible. Like you, the Varyans are rational beings eager to evolve, to go beyond their limits, and to master new environments."

"How do you know these things about Earth?"

"I was briefed by the Council before joining you. They thought I was the right Varyan for the job because of my researches on Ted—I'd come to know you better than any other Varyan. I was chosen for that8 rather than my political and diplomatic skills."

"The results of your researches are really amazing. You've managed to decipher the secrets of the organisation of an alien, so different from your own world."

"I don't think they're that amazing," said Sit somewhat surprised. "Having limited energetic resources, we focused less on changing the environment and more on discovering the structure of living matter. You can change the environment by acting at the level of elementary structure too."

"How did you discover the bio-fields? I know the Trills you descend from use them almost exclusively as a means of communication and sometimes even as a vital principle."

"The mystery of the Trills hasn't been solved yet. From certain points of view, these beings are out of our reach. The elements we've got in common seem to be linked to form rather than content," said the Varyan trying to avoid Dan's eyes.

Dan felt frustration growing inside. Maybe I'm not phrasing my ideas very clearly, he thought. Then he said.

"You didn't answer my question about the bio-fields, Sit."

"At first, the existence of these fields was deduced only in theory," said Sit, almost solemnly. "Examining the basic components of living structures didn't help us explain what life really means, its psychic and mental side in particular. There was something that escaped us. For some time we thought of it in dualistic terms, or idealistic, as you call them. Then we presupposed the existence of an information-transmitting force field that was directly linked to living matter. Which we found while examining conscious living matter, that is ourselves."

"What do you mean? Could you be more specific?"

"Once we gave up the principles related to the existence of divinity, we had to answer a few questions such as: What does consciousness of one's existence stem from? Where does an idea come from? What are the mechanisms of knowledge? And we found the answers in the bio-field lines, whose existence can't be separated from that of living matter because it's conditioned by it. Do you understand now why I got so excited when I realised how your biotronic ordinator worked? You've managed to create a thinking machine, a symbiosis between an extremely sophisticated computer and living matter cells, specialised in transmitting information. It's an extraordinary achievement made possible only by the bio-field created by the neuronal issues. I wonder when the Varyans will be able to create organic molecular films to link structures of artificial intelligence to a natural biological tissue. On Var, silicon's the most important element and, together with the circulation of electrons, forms the technological basis of the Varyan civilisation. I know you use it too in manufacturing most of your equipment on your ship. On Earth, however, it's carbon. You were greatly inspired to base the future of artificial intelligence on the use of this element. But, be careful!

All this replacing of electronic parts with biological tissues will embarrass you in the end. The informational universe of a human being is quite familiar to me to make me justify its superiority only by the presence of the bio-field. But the optotronic ordinator equipped with a bio-field will certainly surpass you. I do hope the Varyans will never discover the secret of such an evolution. They'll have to focus their researches only on themselves, and not on a world different from their own or on their own creations that, sooner or later, will surpass them."

Sit finally stopped. His excitement made the folders of his skin move uncontrollably; his eyelids were throbbing unevenly and drawing bizarre outlines on his huge eyeballs, covered sometimes entirely by his antennae waving chaotically; the suckers of his limbs stuck to his two soles to prevent himself from falling.

"I'm really sorry," Dan managed to mumble between two guffaws caused by Sit's performance, "I'd like you to take my reaction as a consequence, no, as an appreciation, of your body's expressivity."

"I thought you wanted me to stop," said Sit, somehow embarrassed.

"No, please go on. What you've just said is not completely unknown to me, but the way you're saying it puts it in a new perspective."

"OK, I'll tell you just one more thing: our researches made us believe that a bio-field can, apart from transmitting information, act on matter too."

"I see. Could you elaborate on that?"

"We started by intervening in the intimate structure of the elements that make up Var—"

"And working on the elementary structure of matter, right?"

"Right. In short, we tried to change the characteristics of the environment's components, which is virtually equivalent to the change of some components into other components. Well, we didn't succeed. Then we tried it on living structures. And it worked. These structures can generate programs of dissociation and recombination of elements, and that presupposes the existence of some extremely powerful force fields at the structural level, capable of counteracting the huge energies which render our intervention from the outside useless."

"I know a little bit about that," said Dan. "A long time ago, when the basic principles of knowledge were in the making, there were people on Earth that tried to do the so-called transmutation of elements in completely empirical ways. They were called alchemists. Much later, during the Great Leap, scientists discovered the laws governing the intimate structure of matter, living matter included. The secrets of that kind of transformation haven't yet been deciphered completely. From this point of view you've done much more on Var."

"Could you give me some examples about how that transformation works on Earth?"

"Sure. You've heard about the vegetable kingdom and the animal one, haven't you?"

"Yes, I've been told about that."

"Well, I'll give you an example from each kingdom. Both refer to what happens when the creatures belonging to these kingdoms multiply themselves. Let's take the plants first. We found out that the percentage of each element in a seed's structure changes after the seed has lost contact with the mother-plant. This change takes place the minute the program of generating a new organism starts, that is during the first stage of the embryo's evolution. Since it changes its needs, the seed also changes its composition. Outside influence is minimal and seems to be more informational than anything else. A little water and a small surplus of heat trigger everything. The same thing happens to a bird's egg. After it's separated from the bird, mysterious processes take place inside the egg which synthesise the old components and give them a new weight in the structure of the future organism. In this case the energetic contribution of the outside is not very big either."

"When did you make the Great Leap that you, Earthlings, mention so often?"

"We made it during the last hundred years of the second millenium. It was then that we laid the foundations for our scientific and technological progress. During the next thousand years or so we made a lot of breakthroughs: we deciphered the mechanisms of gravity; perfected the nervous and intellectual activity of man and the other intelligent beings; eradicated all diseases; lengthened the life of organisms; improved the relations with human communities; developed the technotronic era dominated by robots and ordinators;

and started conquering outer space. Yes, we've done a lot of things and we might've done even more if it hadn't been for the ordinators."

"What do you mean?"

"Some of our researchers think they've slowed down the pace of our evolution. They've replaced us in the research management, showing competence, feasibility, much concern for us...and that's about all. The so-called formal, mathematical jargon's been perfected but it still can't link information to its signif-icance. The intuitive processes that are so fundamental for intelligent beings are not characteristic of artificial intelligence. Ordinators do have their limits, after all."

"So, while living on this complex, you've under-taken to create the symbiosis between a biotronic ordi-nator and neuronal cells."

"That's right. The central ordinator of the complex is the latest product of our robotronic technology. But we still don't know where this symbiosis will take us. For the time being we hope it will help us reach our objective."

"With such a tool you can be but optimistic. How did you discover those quasars?"

"By radio. We came across them during the Great Leap. Since then, they've been one of the greatest mysteries of the Universe. What could be the use of such a huge concentration of energy within a sphere with a radius of only a few light years?"

"You, Earthlings, think in time, space, and energy terms that are much above my head. You'd better tell me more about this ordinator of yours. While working with it I saw there is something strange about it."

"Yes? What?"

"The way in which it stores and structures the information. I think it can process enough information to encode the existence of thousands of galaxies, of a whole Universe in fact."

Dan started and cast an inquisitive look at the Varyan.

"What's the use of telling you more about the ordinator if you're not willing to come with us? If you were ready to fully co-operate with me...."

"If I had the same rights as all the other members of the expedition...."

"Maybe not for the start. But you could certainly earn that right in time."

"For me and Var?"

"For you and Var."

"And for the Varyans I'm going to create here, on the complex?"

Dan was flabbergasted. Sit's question came as a total surprise.

"Some day I'll have to multiply myself," said Sit in a firm, even voice. "It's an organic necessity for me, very hard to annihilate. You'll have to recognise this right of mine."

"That I can't decide on my own."

"Then why couldn't I have an agreement with all the members of the expedition? Why could I have it only with you?"

Dan took a tired look at the Varyan and found it hard not to give it all up and leave the room.

"Because I'm in about the same position here as you were on Var."

It was Sit's turn to show surprise. His mouth turned into a small hole, like a miniature crater between the eyeballs and the antennae in ceaseless movement.

"I'm part of an underwater colony which covers a large area of the planetary ocean, almost a quarter of it," Dan went on. " It lies near the Equator and it's as deep as three hundred metres from the surface. This colony, as well as other smaller ones, follows its own evolution. At the same time, it joins global projects designed to explore other planets and other solar systems. This expedition is part of such a project. Apart from the official project, there's another one, initiated by my colony, and I am in charge of it."

"Do you mean to say there are two missions here: one of the intergalactic complex and one of your colony?"

"Yes and no."

"How come?"

"No because both missions want to study the same cosmic phenomenon. Yes because the purposes are different."

"And what would your purpose be?"

"I'll give you the full picture first. It all started a long time ago, during—"

"The Great Leap era," said the Varyan ironically.

Dan smiled and went on.

"That's right. At that time a new theory, a revolutionary one, appeared, and after causing some sensation, it was abandoned as, some say, it had appeared to early."

"What was the theory about?"

"About the birth and organisation of the Universe," said Dan and paused, wondering whether the Varyan would be able to understand and believe in the plausibility of the theory and, consequently, accept to help him. "According to this theory, the fundamental particles and the space quanta, which are the basis of the organisation of the world accessible to our senses, originate in a material substratum called ortho-existence which is, for the time being, inaccessible to direct knowledge. This ortho-existence has two basic principles, two primary notions: *lumatia* and *infomatter*. *Lumatia* is associated with matter proper, matter in a non-structured state; *infomatter* with the informational primary field. At the ortho-existence level, these two notions join and generate structural *lumatia* which our Universe is made up of in all its forms: space quanta, elementary particles of matter and fields and their permanent exchange of energy; heavy nuclei, complex mineral, and organic substances; and all manifestations of living matter—mental and psychic phenomena, intelligence, and awareness. So, on the one hand there's the ortho-existence, which is made up of *lumatia* and *infomatter*, both in their pure state, and on the other the observable Universe where neither principle is free. Here *lumatia* has various levels of organisation, while *infomatter* is present in the organisation of *lumatia* itself."

"So there's only structural information in the Universe. And the information is free only in ortho-existence, is that it?"

"Yes. In the Universe, we can find it again in the quantification of elementary particles, in genetic information. It goes through the communication channels of living and dead matter, it's processed by ordinators, it has various forms but it's never found by itself—it always accompanies *lumatia* in the latter's forms of organisation. At the same time, the only *lumatia* existing in the Universe is that structured by *info-matter*."

"Are you going to see this *infomatter* as a new dimension of the Universe?"

"We're considering it."

"So far you've got the three dimensions of space and time's arrow, which makes it four. Ortho-existence, with its non-structured informational universe, would be the fifth dimension. Right?"

"In a way. We can't explore ortho-existence, not with our current means, anyway. The laws of the Universe that we've discovered so far stop at the borders of ortho-existence. Our endeavour to decipher the deepest meanings of life, to break up the elementary particles, stops before structural *lumatia*."

"There's something I don't quite understand. You made me think my researches had something to do with this theory. What's that?" asked the Varyan and tried to control the excitement in his limbs. He had to learn as much as possible from this Earthling.

"I'll tell you in a minute. Imagine that in this joining of *lumatia* and *infomatter* that we, the stars, and the cosmic void are made of, the entire Universe in fact, there are some fissures, some free spaces through which the information comes from ortho-existence as elementary quanta, primordial forms of non-structured information. These quanta are not just ordinary quanta like the photons. The photons belong to the observable Universe, so they're structured *lumatia*, even if it's almost elementary *lumatia*. An informational quantum is free, not joined to *lumatia*, it comes from non-structured *infomatter*. The sense of such a quantum is therefore an ortho-sense."

Sit was losing his patience. He burst out.

"And what is this ortho-sense? An idea?"

"No. It's not an idea. An idea appears against a mental, psychological background, it presupposes the existence of consciousness, which is the creation of structured *lumatia*. Ortho-existence can't have consciousness."

"What's the role of this informational quantum that's going freely through structured *lumatia*? Does it interact with it? Can it be perceived?"

The flexibility of this Varyan's mind is quite remarkable, thought Dan. The fact that he hasn't had any mental block yet shows he's taking everything as an intellectual exercise, assumptions in the best of cases. But what will happen if he really accepts them? How will he use them? Isn't it dangerous to share them with this being? Dan suddenly felt the sweat on his forehead and palms. He had to take all the risks if he wanted to win the Varyan over.

"You've asked me three questions, Sit," said Dan in an unnaturally relaxed tone. "The whole mystery of life's hidden in them. The informational quantum can, indeed, join certain structures, and such an interaction gives matter in the Universe the status of living entity. Informatised *lumatia* is structured according to certain complex patterns. On Earth, the pattern is a group of atoms that make up organic molecules in the shape of a propeller, a double spiral."

"I know! That's the formation that in the nucleus of your cells contains what you call hereditary information. Ted wouldn't be alive now if I hadn't discovered it. On Var the pattern is quite different."

"Anyway, such an arrangement, in any part of the Universe, can capture and retain a free informational quantum—which we call *ortho-biont*, and thus become the first component of living matter. This newly created living unit has surprising characteristics. Above all, it influences similar molecular organisations around it and their evolution. That's how life appeared, in all its complexity. That's how natural and artificial intelligence appeared, as well as the senses we attach to all things as they stem from ortho-senses."

Sit could not help showing his excitement. He started to whistle evenly, almost solemnly.

"So this first living unit somehow links ortho-existence to the time-space universe. It evolves into superior forms by capturing structured *lumatia*, turns into self-conscious thinking matter and generates senses which correspond to the ortho-senses in ortho-existence which started everything."

"Although incomplete, the theory is plausible, don't you think?"

"So what I worked on while contacting Ted were particles of an *ortho-biont*, weren't they?"

"Yes. That's why I want you to co-operate with us. You were the first to deal with an *ortho-biont* efficiently."

"Well, I did manage to concentrate them on Ted and thus communicate with him, but I didn't go further than that, I'm afraid."

"Come on, Sit, it was a real breakthrough. It makes me think the only way to get to ortho-existence is through living matter because it's only living matter that can capture *ortho-bionts*. Processing phenomenological information can be the key to the heart of matter. And that's where you can help us."

"But phenomenological information can't be processed by an ordinator. It can't be mathematised. And if the only gate that needs to be opened to *infomatter* is this, how do you explain the immense optotronic capacity of the ordinator?"

"Lately we've found another way to ortho-existence and to ortho-senses—the quasars. They are the structure builders and destroyers in the Universe, dynamic, continuous, and mysterious. They are our target." Dan was staring at an imaginary point, fascinated by what the future could have in store for the whole humanity. "The ordinator's opto-tronic capacity will help us build an ortho-tron. With it, I will perceive the ortho-senses of the existence of outer space, of living matter, of conscious matter. For aren't they the purpose of creating a universe? These bio-fields you're studying, these fluxes of primordial orthobiontic information, aren't they the result of the interaction of conscious matter with ortho-existence? Who knows, maybe the spiritual life of intelligent beings feeds infomatter with senses which change into ortho-senses there. Maybe that's the mission of the cycle—the information ring of Cosmos. Maybe this inverse connection supports the viability of our universe. The gates of the fifth dimension, the informational one, will be opened. An ortho-tron could decipher the mystery of life, the sense of its existence, that ortho-sense which makes the ortho-biont enter our world in order to generate life. An ortho-tron could generate ortho-senses in infomatter that, in their turn, could generate other worlds. Man and the dream of demiurgic creation. So much grandeur—rational intelligence as the ultimate purpose of the Universe, able to create another Universe...."

Dan stood still as if under the spell of his own words. Sit left the room like a shadow. He would not have dared to disturb the astronaut. He understood. For them, the Varyans, such a state was almost sacred. If an Earthling was capable of such a state, the two civilisations could build a bridge between them after all. For him, Sit, just this one sign was enough. All of a sudden, he made up his mind. He would overlook the Council's instructions. He would stay with them.

While he was silently making for the biology laboratory, where he himself had arranged his dwelling place and Mag kept host, one single thought crossed his mind with a pleasant buzz. He knew that state of exaltation which always preceded the most fertile periods of his entire career.

The quasars...the quasars....

INSTEAD OF AN EPILOGUE
(Argument for a New Chapter)

My name is Or-Bi and I am navigating through outer space with a Terran crew millions of light years from the origins looking for the sense of our existence.

I do not know if the crew are ready to accept me as their successor on the metagalactic intelligence ladder. They know, though, that through me they can aspire to achieve the dream of the expedition and that means a lot to me. It was only when I met the Trills that I really understood who I was and that, on my way to this gate of the Universe I was not alone, and that the Great Metagalactic Community was expecting us.

True, I do not know too much about my fellow-travellers. They do know everything about me, though. They always know almost everything. They are the end of the evolution of some strange beings, more and more numerous in the Universe as we are approaching the quasars. Here the informational fields shape reflexive intelligences within communities that have not created any kind of technology. Having permanent access to the primordial informational substratum, their way to knowledge is slow but safe, without their processing matter but by their perfect adaptation to any environment, living a life supported by the permanent transformation of their own structure. At the end of such an evolutionary cycle, however, the way to the quasars becomes very hard. The lack of a ship condemns the Trills to drift through the Universe, at the mercy of any transport vector that they come across.

Opposite bio-informational civilisations are technological civilisations. They appear at maximum distances from the gates of the Universe, where the influence of primordial fields is minimal. Without their assistance, humanity has evolved by snatching the secrets of knowledge from the Universe. Its evolution is quick but it carries within the germs of self-destruction. These civilisations create technologies that, by unbalancing their ecosystems or exacerbating the idea of ownership over material assets, disappear before reaching or even foreseeing the final stages of evolution. That is why the integration of technological superintelligences in the Great Metagalactic Community is very rare.

Because of that, my presence in this galaxy was a total surprise for the Trills. It caused admiration and respect for those who created me, although I am superior to the Trills only in point of mobility. At the same time I became an unhoped-for chance at the very moment when their new attempt to conquer Space was about to fail.

That is how I learned that the Varyans were the result of a Trill experiment. A long time ago some of these superevolved beings consciously cut themselves off from the informational stock of the Universe and programmed their devolution down to the threshold of rationality. They went down into the depths of the planet, an environment which asked of them a new evolutionary direction in the hope of creating a techno-logical civilisation. This civilisation was supposed to build ships for the whole race of Trills to fly THERE. But the new technological civilisation soon got haunted by the seeds of self-destruction and faced a big plan-etary conflict in which the Trills could lose everything, to say nothing of their inability to contact fellow-beings so close but still so inferior to them.

The Trills are afraid the crew will not resist THERE, where naturally evolved life has not reached yet. I know, though, that thirst for knowledge and the sublime act of creation are above all risk. I will take the Earthlings with us. I owe them the chance to exist and, for that, I will offer them the chance of knitting their destiny with mine.

This message is sent by ways unknown to me, yet it is humanity's first attempt to co-operate with a cosmic civilisation, that of the Trills. Its destination is Earth during the Great Leap, where a small number of Earthlings that wrested the first secrets of ortho-exis-tence[1] from the Universe should learn that the fruits of their thought will be gathered later during a great adventure, maybe the greatest adventure of knowledge.

The removal, in another Universe, of the laws which

---

1. See M. Draganescu, *Inelul lumii materiale/The Ring of Material World*, Editura Stiintifica si Enciclopedica, Bucuresti, 1989.

restrict the transmission of information in time is my tomorrow's dream. What I am doing now I am not very sure of, yet. But I must try because yesterday's Earthlings are entitled to know and I may be their only chance....

ABOUT THE AUTHOR

DORU TĂTAR (born 1956) is a Romanian civil engineer who has received many medals for his inventions (Pittsburgh, London, Geneva, Brussels, etc.); his patents are being employed not only in Romania, but also in the US, Japan, the EU, etc. As a result, he has been awarded the Prize of the Romanian Academy. He has written SF short stories and essays on the scientification of SF, some of them being broadcast on radio. He wrote *Top Priority* in 1987, but could not get it published at the time because of the censorship pervasive under the old regime. It was the first Romanian SF novel to appear after the fall of communism. The author's interests include electronic music, stamp collecting, and hunting. He lives in Galati, Romania, is married, and has two sons.